lost property

James Moloney has worked at a fruit market and in a truck factory but it was his experience as a young teacher in western Queensland that led to his early novels, *Crossfire*, *Dougy* and *Gracey*. His short novel *Swashbuckler* won the Children's Book Council of Australia Book of the Year Award in 1996 and in the following year, *A Bridge to Wiseman's Cove* was named Book of the Year in the CBCA's Older Readers category. His other titles have appeared regularly on shortlists for literary prizes and children's choice awards ever since.

'I like to get inside the head of today's adolescents, to connect with the passion they have for life and understand what they care about. The challenge then is to express it in a story. That challenge keeps me young. I love it.'

James and his wife, Kate, live in Brisbane with their three children.

Also by James Moloney

The Book of Lies
Black Taxi
Touch Me
Crossfire
Dougy
Gracey
The House on River Terrace
A Bridge to Wiseman's Cove
Angela

lost property

JAMES MOLONEY

VIKING
an imprint of
PENGUIN BOOKS

VIKING

Published by the Penguin Group
Penguin Group (Australia)
250 Camberwell Road, Camberwell, Victoria 3124, Australia
(a division of Pearson Australia Group Pty Ltd)
Penguin Group (USA) Inc.
375 Hudson Street, New York, New York 10014, USA
Penguin Group (Canada)
90 Eglinton Avenue East, Suite 700,
Toronto ON M4P 2Y3, Canada
(a division of Pearson Penguin Canada Inc.)
Penguin Books Ltd
80 Strand, London WC2R 0RL, England
Penguin Ireland
25 St Stephen's Green, Dublin 2, Ireland
(a division of Penguin Books Ltd)
Penguin Books India Pvt Ltd
11 Community Centre, Panchsheel Park, New Delhi – 110 017, India
Penguin Group (NZ)
Cnr Airborne and Rosedale Roads, Albany, Auckland, New Zealand
(a division of Pearson New Zealand Ltd)
Penguin Books (South Africa) (Pty) Ltd
24 Sturdee Avenue, Rosebank, Johannesburg 2196, South Africa

Penguin Books Ltd, Registered Offices: 80 Strand, London, WC2R 0RL, England

First published by Penguin Group (Australia), a division of Pearson Australia Group Pty Ltd, 2005

10 9 8 7 6 5 4 3 2

Text copyright © James Moloney, 2005

Designed by Marina Messiha © Penguin Group (Australia)
Cover photograph by Steve Vaccariello/ photolibrary.com
Typeset in 11/17pt Berkeley Oldstyle by Post Pre-Press Group, Brisbane, Queensland
Printed in Australia by McPherson's Printing Group, Maryborough, Victoria

National Library of Australia
Cataloguing-in-Publication data:

Moloney, James.
Lost property.

ISBN-13: 978 0 670 02943 3.
ISBN-10: 0 670 02943 2.

I. Title

A823.4

www.penguin.com.au

Acknowledgements

I would like to offer special thanks to my wife, Kate Moloney, and to Leonie Tyle, Daniel Farrington, Dominic Miller and Samuel McCarthy for their help during the writing of Lost Property.

For Cath Collier and Jenny Johns

Happiness is not a goal, it's a by-product

Eleanor Roosevelt

I first saw the woman when she stopped some way ahead of me in the crowd, forcing others to step around her as though she were a stubborn stone blocking the stream. Her solitary figure seemed dwarfed by the station's massive roof, which trapped the fetid December air and surrounded her with echoes from the trains and the birds that nested high on the ribcage of rafters and especially the people, so many milling, preoccupied people. She stared back in my direction for a moment and that brief glance was enough. Only three days in the job but the solemn face and the anxious stoop of her shoulders were already familiar. This woman was another customer for Clive and me.

She looked around, intimidated, but not yet lost. Someone must have given her directions: 'Central Station, at the Pitt Street end of the main concourse, opposite Platform One. Just look for the sign, *Lost Property*.'

The woman was still getting her bearings when I pushed

through the heavy doors into the Lost Property Office and went down the curved ramp that brought our customers to us. Another door, this one marked *Staff Only* stood to the left. I punched in the security code, shouldered my way inside and called, 'Clive, I'm back.'

'Good, Josh. Can you watch the counter?' the muffled voice replied from inside the compactus where most of the lost property was kept.

My dad had arranged this job for me through his contacts at work; one of his many grateful clients was a supervisor for City Rail. Mr Bale was his name, and a week before school finished he called me in for an interview.

'A bloke in Lost Property is going off on his honeymoon,' he told me. 'You know your way around a computer, don't you?'

'Sure. How long's he away for?' I asked. Didn't want to work the whole holidays.

'Four weeks.' And then Mr Bale told me what I'd be paid.

'Great, where do I sign?'

He'd grunted and shoved a complicated form across the table at me. 'You'll be working with Clive. He'll show you what to do.'

The computer sat off-centre on the wide counter. A random stab at the keyboard brought the screen to life, but before I could enter any data from the forms piled beside it, the woman I'd seen earlier came silently down the ramp and stopped a metre or so short. Not a bad guess, eh! We stared at each other through the thick perspex screen that left only a twenty centimetre gap above the laminex. She leaned forward and spoke into the gap as though it was a microphone set too low on a podium.

'Can you help me, please? I've come about a cardigan. I think I left it on the train last week. They said at my local station that you might have it here.'

'A cardigan. What colour was it, Madam?'

Madam! Would you listen to me; since when did I ever say stuff like that? But Clive had insisted, it was one of the first things he told me on Monday morning, 'Be polite. Call the men, "Sir", and the women, "Madam".'

'Blue, navy blue,' said the woman. 'With gold buttons,' she added as an afterthought, dipping even lower towards that gap to be sure I heard her.

I set to work on the computer, calling up a new query screen and choosing 'Jumper/cardigan' from the pull-down menu.

'We'll need to know what train you were on and the date of the journey.'

These questions were part of the procedure Clive had taught me along with standard words like 'item' and 'proof of identity'. After a few more questions I moved to the 'search' box and gave the mouse a firm tap with my index finger.

Bingo, we had a match. *Dark-blue cardigan with two gold buttons,*' I read from the screen. 'Handed in at Campbelltown last Tuesday. I'll go and find it for you.'

I walked round behind the head-high wall that shielded the compactus. 'Clive, I've got a match. Need to open Bay Five.'

Out of the corner of my eye I glimpsed his stout figure emerge from between the open shelves of the compactus. My hands were already on the first of the wheels, black and about the size of a steering wheel, that rolled the heavy shelves along the rails. Call me a big kid, but I loved this part of the job.

When Bay Five lay open before me, I stepped into the compactus and began my search. Clive wandered closer until he stood in the passageway, watching me. 'What's the customer after, Josh?'

'Woman's cardigan.'

'Further along and one level down then.'

There it was, navy blue and, as the clincher, gold buttons. I stepped past Clive and back to the counter.

'Here it is, Madam,' I said, cringing inwardly at my own formality.

As soon as I pushed the cardigan under the screen, she snatched it away and held it out before her, examining it front and back with the eye of a forensic scientist. But after she'd repeated the process twice more, her arms fell limp by her side leaving the cardigan trailing with one sleeve on the floor. It was like watching a balloon lose all of its air. Her heavy make-up couldn't hide the deep creases in her face any more and tears glistened around the rims of her eyes. She didn't say a word, she couldn't, but her gasping breath and the downcast head spoke loudly enough.

It must be the wrong one, but why would anyone get so upset over a cardigan? Silent seconds ticked by. I should say something to her, but what? Then, before the cogs in my mind could crank out the right words, the security door opened and Clive was at the woman's side.

'Would you like to come in for a moment? There's a chair you can sit on.'

The woman turned towards him, still mute, and let him usher her into the office. My first thought was, hey, this is wrong. On Monday, when Clive was laying down the law, rule one was 'Be polite' and rule two was 'Don't let anyone through that door'. Yet here he was, sitting the woman down at the circular table where the two of us ate our lunches.

'Would you like a cup of tea? I have some in the thermos,' he said, nodding towards the centre of the table.

She refused this offer but accepted a glass of water. The coldness in her throat seemed to bring back her voice. 'I don't like to be such a nuisance. You're very kind to let me sit down like this.' And she put the cardigan on the table in front of her without even looking at it.

'I'm sorry this wasn't the one you were looking for.' I moved closer and reached down to pick it up but she dropped her hand firmly on top to stop me.

'Oh, this is the one,' she said sadly, draping it over her arm. 'Hardly need it on a day like today, do I? That was it, you see. It had been cool when I set out from home last week but by the afternoon it was hot in the train. I must have taken it off without thinking and because the weather has been so warm ever since, I haven't needed it. It was only yesterday, when I hadn't seen it for days, that I . . .'

Tears were welling up in her eyes again and her voice

faltered. What was happening here? She had her cardigan back, didn't she? I couldn't work this lady out.

'It wasn't the cardigan you came looking for, was it?' said Clive.

The woman took a second sip from the glass, then, sitting up straighter in her chair, she closed her eyes and let the tears roll freely onto her cheeks and down to the corners of her trembling mouth. 'There was a brooch. It wasn't worth much. I doubt a jeweller would give you a hundred dollars for it.'

'Sentimental value,' said Clive gently.

She nodded. 'A gift from my grandmother, from her silver wedding anniversary. My grandfather was killed just a year after he gave it to her, an accident. That brooch meant so much to her. They were going to bury it with her when she died, but she'd left instructions in a letter to her daughter, my mother, that she wanted it to stay in the family and be worn every day if the occasion suited. Those were her words. I still have the letter.'

The story became too much; the woman's head drooped forward and she began to sob with deep, painful jerks that almost threw her from the chair. 'How will I live with myself . . . my own carelessness . . . the brooch is lost to the family.'

Clive pulled out the other chair and sat close by, facing her around the rim of the table. He didn't stretch out his hand to touch her and he didn't seem any better at comforting words than I was but his presence made a difference. The woman hauled herself back until she was sitting upright in the chair again and managed to stop the sobbing.

'It was too much to hope for, I suppose. When people find something like that on a train, they would think nothing of . . .'

'Not always,' said Clive and then he called to me over his shoulder, 'Josh, did you check the flag?'

This might seem an odd thing to say but he wasn't talking about something that flaps in the breeze. I knew immediately what he meant and felt a heavy stone sink into my gut.

The woman was confused by this talk of a flag but she was sharp enough to guess there might still be hope. She looked at Clive, asking for an explanation without uttering a word.

'Sometimes we separate items when they are handed in, especially jewellery. All valuables go into the safe.'

I was already hurrying back to the computer as he spoke. There it was, a box at the bottom of the screen telling me to click here for a cross-reference.

'There's a flag,' I called to Clive.

'What number?' The direction of his voice meant that he was waiting in front of the safe, a brutal grey-metal thing about the size of a fridge that stood in the far corner. I clicked with the mouse and read the number aloud off the screen. Heard him mutter, 'Here we are.'

Both of us arrived back at the table together. The woman was on her feet and desperate to see what he was holding in his hand.

'Oh my goodness, my grandmother's brooch.' She was on it like a cat after a mouse. 'Thank you, oh, thank . . .'

She didn't quite get the last word out because the tears

were back, tears of relief this time. She had struggled unsuc-
cessfully to suppress them earlier, in her misery, but now she
didn't bother. There was no hugging or jumping about, but
an unreserved joy was radiating out of her. If we'd turned off
the lights she would have glowed like one of those luminous
statues of the Virgin Mary.

Through it all, she clutched the precious brooch to her
chest, stealing a look at it every second or two. 'I thought it
was lost,' she whispered. 'Lost forever.'

It was a few minutes after five when I started on my way home,
down the escalator and into the swirling crowd coming up
from Eddy Street, past the fruit stall and the florist with it's
gaudy Christmas lights and into the tunnels that led to the
trains. On board, I hung from a strap near the doors, hemmed
in by listless bodies on every side as the wheels clanged and
shuddered across a set of points. Then the acceleration forced
a stiffening of the legs and a tighter grip on the strap, until the
faint stench of burning brakes drifted into the carriage and we
came to a halt at the next station.

It had been the same on Monday and Tuesday, but today,
instead of dinner or a cold drink or the cricket score from the
Test Match in Adelaide, I found myself thinking about that
woman. It was the way she had wept and then the euphoria in
her face, like some figure in a Renaissance masterpiece.

The press of bodies around me gradually thinned out and
after Kogarah there was even a spare seat. I sat down and fitted
the ear plugs of my iPod into place but instead of the words

and the heavy beat, I heard that woman again and saw her face. She was so happy, so free, so alive. That's a great feeling, a moment of happiness when there is no holding back, nothing in the way and every bit of joy can get through to the surface, shining out of you like that woman's face. I remember the sensation from years ago, Primary School maybe, though there was no single day I could pick out as special. I just remember feeling it.

chapter two

The train pulled into Oatley where I stepped off and began the last kilometre of my journey. An easy walk without a school bag to carry, though the sun still packed a sting and my shirt was sticking to my skin in places by the time I slipped down the shady path beside our house. My mother was hopping from one leg to the other in the kitchen doorway.

'Guess what came in the mail today, Josh,' she said, waving a large envelope. School's crest in the corner. I had been sweating on that envelope for a couple of weeks now.

Mum backed into the kitchen, making me follow her. She likes bright colours and absolutely refuses to wear brown because it was the uniform at Our Lady's when she went to school. Today, she was in a lime green top and a knee-length skirt to match. As always, Aunty Joanne's gold bangle flopped on her wrist. Mum works for a radio station, part-time mostly. 'My other job is taxidriver for you lot,' she's always telling

Hayley and me, but years ago she had a spot on-air, interviewing sportsmen for the ABC, sort of 'the woman's angle' and that was how she met Dad.

She was still holding the envelope, teasing me, so I snatched it from her, a quick movement she didn't even see coming. She let out a gasp of surprise and then a laugh, but the moment of shock in her eyes left me wishing I hadn't done it. It was a reminder that my mother was so much shorter than me, with the gap growing wider every time a new pencil mark was made on the doorjam between the kitchen and the dining room. A different kind of uneasiness sometimes made me think Mum was actually shrinking but I put that thought aside for now.

A quick rip at the envelope and the pages slipped into my hand, a separate one for each subject. Ignoring the marks, I flicked down through the pile until there it was, the last page of the lot, a certificate with the words – *Entitled to an Honour Pocket for Academic Excellence*. It was my first.

Time to relax now and look at the marks at a more leisurely pace. There was Modern History, third in the pile. Yes! I did a mental fist-clench at the plus sign after the A. Mr Habden had been taunting me all year, the devious bastard. 'You're good enough, Josh, if you would only use that brain God gave you.'

Mum took the reports from my hand and, to the music of the saucepans bubbling away behind her, devoured each page.

'Oh, Josh, you've done so well.'

She'd lingered over the certificate at the bottom, but didn't know what it meant until I told her. My older brother Michael wasn't the academic type.

Dad's car pulled into the garage – must be half-past six. My father sells Holdens. Mum joked once that he wanted to name me after the cars he loves so much. It might have worked – Holden Tambling. Instead they settled on Joshua teamed with Terence for a middle name in honour of Terry Vickers, an old coach down at Kogarah Oval who helped Dad break into the big-time. My father played Rugby League for the mighty St George Dragons and people still remember him, even though he retired twenty years ago. These days his name helps to sell cars.

'Call Hayley for dinner would you, Josh,' said Mum.

My little sister was on her bed reading Harry Potter for the seventeenth time, but she'd heard Mum and was already stirring her long legs when I poked my head round the corner. Hayley inherited Dad's sporting talents – the ones that passed me by. Not even thirteen and she could swim fifty metres in the time it took me to do twenty-five. Even as a seven-year-old she didn't hold back when we wrestled Dad for the remote, the three of us on the carpet grunting and squealing until a stray leg banged into the furniture and Mum would shout from the kitchen, 'Go outside if you're going to be so rough.'

Before that, it was Michael who wrestled Dad, with me joining in where I could. Had to be careful because the two of them went at it like a couple of bears, grunting and laughing.

I don't mind that Michael and Hayley got all the sporting

genes. Music's more my go. My mates and I have put a band together.

By the time Hayley and I reached the dining room, Dad was in his place at the head of the table reading my report. He's not big, as footballers go – 184 centimetres, the same as me. A lot of ex-sporting types stack on the kilos once they retire but my father has actually lost weight. These days, people describe him as cadaverous, like Christopher Lee in a vampire movie. The grey hair doesn't help and there's not as much of that as there used to be.

'Wonderful, Josh, congratulations,' he said. 'You deserve it, too, after all the work you put in this year.' He leaned back while Hayley placed a steaming bowl in front of him.

'Read the comments, Phil,' Mum called once she was settled in her place. 'The business about contributing in class.'

Spare me! This could get embarrassing.

'A thoughtful student always willing to share his ideas,' Dad read from the page for Study of Religion.

'Did you hear that?' cried Mum in mock indignation as she sat down at her end of the table. 'Your teachers wouldn't say that if they'd been watching you around this house lately.'

Parents want everything, don't they? It's not good enough to get five As from six subjects, but I have to be Mr Chat Show as well.

Dad read from the next sheet, Modern History. 'Contributes freely to discussions in class,' said Dad, quoting Mr Habden's words. Habden had joked that he was going to write, *Likes the sound of his own voice.*

Before Dad could go any further, the phone rang. His eyes went straight to his wristwatch and right away I guessed what he was thinking. Hayley was already on her feet and heading into the kitchen.

'Leave it for Josh,' Mum called. She was thinking the same thing.

My sister came back into the dining room disappointed, but she could read faces as well as I could and sat down without complaint.

I pushed back my chair and went past her into the kitchen.

'Josh Tambling,' I said as soon as I had the cordless to my ear.

'Hi, Josh, it's me.'

The tension left my body and with a hand over the phone, I called into the dining room, 'It's only Alicia.'

Silence, then Mum called, 'Don't be long, Josh. Tell her you'll ring back.'

Alicia was just inviting me over for a swim anyway.

'I'm jamming with the guys tonight, but Steve's place is over near you. What about after that, about nine, maybe.'

That was okay by Alicia. Dad would give me a lift if I asked him, but when I arrived back at the table Mum and Dad had gone quiet, and I knew better than to break that silence just yet.

Dad was playing touch footy in his Over 45s comp as he always did on a Wednesday night and the detour wouldn't take him far out of the way.

'Haven't heard of this guy, Steve, before. What's his last name?'

'Kominsky. He's our new drummer.'

'What happened to the old one?'

'Musical differences.' Like, poor Liam would sound better backing Elton John than Korn, but it was pointless telling Dad that.

'This Steve must have understanding parents if they're going to let you make such a racket in their house.'

'In the garage, Dad. There's just his mother and she works late on Wednesdays.'

'Glad I'm not a neighbour.'

Dad gives me a lot of crap about the band but he bought me the Fender that lay in its case on the back seat. 'We were lucky to find Steve, actually. He's a year behind the rest of us at Fidelis, but his kit's all right and he can keep time better than Liam.'

Steve's garage had been added long after the house was built, jutting out from the end wall and big enough for two cars. Once I was inside, the roller door descended into place and we got down to business.

Meet my band. Neven Vanderoy on lead guitar. His name is Dutch and predicably he has dirty blond hair, but in fact his family came here from South Africa and he still has that odd way of pronouncing some words. His broad shoulders make him look more like a front row forward than a natural on lead guitar. Whenever we jam, he wears T-shirts with the sleeves cut out. 'Gives me more freedom to move,' he claims. Bullshit! Shows off his biceps, more like.

It's a toss-up whether Neven is my best mate or whether that distinction goes to Dave Zilly who plays bass, pretty badly, though he's getting better. Think hollow-chested basketballer for a picture of Dave, and the craters of the moon for his cheeks. No sleeveless T-shirt is ever going to make girls pant for Dave, a fact he faces with a mixture of stoic acceptance and sleazy complaints.

Then there is the new boy, Steve, on drums and finally, at the microphone, with a gleaming red Fender in his hand, Josh Tambling . . . Cue delirium in the mosh pit.

We were working up to our first gig. The recently departed Liam had wanted us to audition for the Fidelis Day concert that was always held early in February, but Neven had howled him down.

'Only wankers play on Fidelis Day. It's all classical guitar and the bloody brass ensemble.'

'They let rappers get up on stage last year,' Liam had countered.

'Hip-hop is shit,' Neven grunted. He was right about that!

Things had been brewing between Neven and Liam right through October and November and this argument had been the last straw. 'They'd let us play if we toned our material down a bit,' Liam shouted.

'We're a serious band!' Neven shouted back.

Now we've got Steve and we're aiming for our first gig at Dave's cousin's eighteenth birthday party. By then we'll have the fire-power we need if an audience is going to take us seriously. That's where my job at the Lost Property Office was so important, because it would take every dollar I earned to buy the second-hand speakers Neven had found at a store in Ultimo.

We do a few covers from bands like Nickelback and my favourite, Bone Jar, but Neven's mostly into cutting-edge stuff that hangs around on the Net. A lot of the songs are anti-war, fight-against-oppression, that sort of thing.

We ran through our growing repertoire and then worked on the new rage-fest Neven had come across from an American band called Body Bag – just a few simple chords, played at a furious pace and the vocals built around a chorus we all shouted at the top of our lungs.

Kill 'em all, kill 'em all,
Do the general's dirty work.
Kill 'em all, kill 'em all,
I'm a gun-toting jerk.

We were still wrenching out the last words when the door connecting the garage to the house opened and a girl appeared. She stayed in the doorway and immediately put her hands to her ears, grimacing until the reverb from the final chords died away.

'Shit, who beat you lot with the angry stick?' she said, once she could be heard. 'Just as well they're not machine-guns you've got in your hands, or I'd be full of holes.'

Not exactly a compliment, but I decided it was more of a comment than a criticism. Who was she, anyway? We all looked towards Steve; if she was his girlfriend, he was doing all right.

'This is my sister, Gemma.' He quickly did the rounds, listing off our names while we looked her over more closely. She was tall for a girl and slim, though certainly not skinny, and judging by the confidence with which she eyed us off in return, she was Steve's older sister. She wore a short denim skirt with a frayed hem and a simple white top, tight where it counted the most. And bare feet too; there's something about a chick with bare feet.

Dave raised an eyebrow as if to say 'not bad' though to be honest, Dave was more likely to say something a little more earthy. Gemma is not a common name and Kominsky certainly isn't. It was ringing a bell with me, and the way she looked directly at me after Steve said my name meant that she felt the same.

'St Catherine's,' she said, beating me to it.

Of course. Gemma Kominsky. We were in the same class in primary school. 'I haven't seen you since the last day of Year Six. How come you don't go to Fidelis, like Steve?'

'Mum had a thing about it. Wanted an all-girls school, so she sent me to Our Lady's instead.'

My memory of Gemma was rushing back, as much as there was to remember, anyway. Some odd words just slipped out before I knew what I was saying. 'You weren't up yourself like the rest of the girls. The way some of them went on, you'd think boys were a stink they'd picked up on their shoes.'

Gemma laughed easily and folded her arms across that

tight white top. 'Yeah, well, you and your mates weren't showing a lot of potential back in Year Six.'

A stifled snigger told me that Neven and Dave were killing themselves at the way she'd skewered me so casually. But she let me off the hook just as quickly. 'Maybe I was hoping you'd end up pretty hot by Year Twelve.'

Was she talking about me? The look on her face made sure the question had no obvious answer, but my mates were practically rolling on the floor by now.

'Josh is hot, all right,' said Dave. 'Just ask Alicia. She melts as soon as he touches her.'

I could have murdered the mongrel.

'Who's Alicia?' asked Gemma with a smirk.

'My girlfriend.' I had to answer, but that didn't stop me exploring her face carefully for a reaction. Um, might have been something there.

We played another song while Gemma pressed her back into the wall, arms folded, swaying her hips and knees a little, though nothing you could call a dance. It wasn't a great song for dancing anyway, with just me singing into the mike on a stand in front of me.

Hungry faces, broken limbs,
I can't take it any more.
Angry, angry, got to change it,
Got to fight before we fall.

'What do you think?' Neven asked, in-your-face as ever.

Gemma shrugged her shoulders. 'Sounds okay, guitars are good. And the drums,' she added when Steve's face dropped a little at being left out of her compliment. 'Didn't like the song much. Are you guys really repressing that much rage?' Again, she had managed to bring us down a peg or two without criticising.

We all looked straight at Neven. 'We don't sing about love and a nice, happy world,' he answered immediately. 'It would be dishonest when there's so much crap going on.'

'Like what?'

He looked surprised that she could question such an obvious truth. 'Poverty, oppression, war.'

She thought about this and shrugged again. 'Not hurting you much, are they? What do you want to shout about them for?'

'It's protest. That's what music's about,' I said, coming to Neven's aid. He might pick most of our songs but I was the one who worked out the chords and the lead line for him to play around with. We were a team.

'Poverty!' said Gemma with a sniff. 'A protest against poverty from guys playing thousand-dollar instruments. Yeah, that makes sense.' She looked at me more squarely now, since I was the one who had taken up the defence. 'What was that song you were singing just now? *I can't take it any more, I'm so angry*,' she mimicked. 'I thought your tonsils were going to pop out.'

'Lay off, Gemma,' Steve demanded.

'I was just asking what he had to be so angry about,' she said, pretending innocence.

'It's just part of the act,' I replied, aware that this wasn't much of a come back.

Neven and I shared a shrug. 'You want to do another one?' he asked.

'No, got to get going.'

Steve's sister obviously felt the same because she disappeared through the doorway as quickly as she'd arrived.

'What'd you think of that?' Neven asked, nodding after her.

I was on my knees, laying the Fender gently inside the velvet lining of its case. 'Like you told her, we don't compromise. Music's got to be honest or it's nothing.'

'No, not that,' said Neven, dropping onto his haunches beside me. He stole a glance over his shoulder towards Dave and Steve then whispered, 'Gemma. What'd you think of the body?'

'Nice feet,' I answered, remembering how the sight of those long legs and shoeless feet had suggested something playful, even sexual.

'Jesus, Josh, there was a lot more to look at than her feet!'

Before I could explain, Dave was towering over us. 'Have you talked your parents round yet?' He had been angling to get me and anyone else who would come up to his sister's house at Port Macquarie for a break before school started. Neven's parents had given the thumbs down, or at least that's what he'd told Dave, so the question was directed at me.

'Pretty much. Mum wasn't so sure at first, but Dad's okay with it and that generally means yes around my place.'

'Sweet, it's on then, as soon as you finish in at the Lost Property Office. Tom rang last night to say he's on board, too,' he added, though he'd told me three times already that Tom Marcovic was coming. 'I can't wait. Seven days of surfing, veging out and watching babes on the beach, with no parents riding shot-gun.'

'Wish I was coming, too,' Neven lamented, with impressive sincerity considering what I suspected about his refusal. He wandered off to put his own guitar away, leaving our appraisal of Gemma Kominsky unfinished.

'Can you give me a lift home?' was Dave's next question.

'Sorry, I'm walking over to Alicia's for a swim.'

'Ah, I lose out to Alicia's curves, do I? She'll be waiting for you in a bikini, I suppose.' His leer said more than his words and I couldn't stop my lips curling into a similar grin.

'I was going to say no when she first asked me round.'

'And then she mentioned the swim, right? That's called advertising your best features.'

I laughed out loud this time because it was so true.

chapter three

Fronting the band was like a work-out in the gym. Hardly surprising, considering the material Neven wants us to play. My throat was raw, my lungs halfway up my neck and the muscles of my stomach and even my legs were aching. An electric guitar was no sack of feathers.

Ah, but the sensation when we all got it right on the same song. There was nothing like it on the footy field. Lately it had been a real buzz belting out the words from deep in the back of my throat, the more ferocious the better. It was as good as punching someone, hitting them with a fist of sound and the raging emotion of the lyrics. I was no fighter but everyone needs a sort of release now and then.

If Steve's sister was hearing my thoughts, I bet she'd say, 'A release from what?' Would have made an interesting conversation. She'd really stuck it to us about the songs we played and she'd found me out in a way, shouting things I didn't believe into the microphone and pretending things that weren't part of my life at all. What she didn't understand was the urge to shout them and the need for the energy they created.

There wasn't a breath of wind in the darkened streets. The summer's night air hung around me like a second damp shirt, making me desperate for a swim by the time I knocked on Alicia's door. It opened almost immediately.

Alicia's face is almost perfectly round with freckles on her nose that she's obsessed with getting rid of. I told her they were cute and she said cute was for dogs and little girls in pigtails.

'Hi, Josh, I was beginning to wonder.'

As she backed away to make room for my guitar case, her dangly earrings swayed to and fro and all the tiny silver shapes on her charm bracelet collided with one another. There was always something moving around Alicia. And she talks a lot. Don't know if I particularly like that about her, but I like the curves that Dave makes such a thing of.

Alicia was in my pastoral group all through Year Eleven – that was how we got together. I wasn't really looking for a girl-friend, but we would meet each day in home-room and joke a bit. There was usually a bunch of us standing round, but she looked at me more than anyone else and laughed at the things I said, in the right kind of way. So we started going out. She told me on the last day of school that it was our four-month anniversary.

Her family called hello to me as we skirted the lounge room. A quick change in the bathroom then it was out through the back of the house to join Alicia by the pool. I could see the strap of her bikini around her neck and trace the outline of the rest under her T-shirt. She pulled the T-shirt quickly over her head and dropped her loose shorts at her feet. Now there was a sight worth all that sweaty walking.

We dived into the pool. There was just the two of us and after three or four laps underwater to cool off, I swam up behind her and put my arm around her waist.

'What do you want?' she asked, pretending to protest. She knew what I wanted. I kissed her under the ear.

She turned around to face me and put her arms around my neck. We were in water up to her shoulder, so it was easy to lose ourselves in the sensation of weightlessness. My hands drifted down the delicious shape of her back to the top of her bikini pants, then slowly, very slowly slipped under the material and kept going.

She pressed her face into the crook of my neck. 'Josh, don't. They can see us from the kitchen window.'

'So we're having a cuddle.'

'More than that, the way you're going,' and she broke away, gliding like a dolphin to the end of the pool. There, she became a sleek and agile seal, hauling herself out of the water in a graceful lunge until she lay on the tiled lip of the pool, turned on her side towards me, her head supported on one hand while the other made sure the pants of her bikini where back where they were supposed to be.

Stroking quickly to the water's edge, I kissed her again, more a peck this time, but her fingers brushed affectionately along my cheek to keep me there. 'That's better,' she murmured.

My attempts to pull her back into the water didn't work. The seal had become a barnacle, so I climbed out and lay head to head with her, flat on my back and with my hands behind my head.

The long silence was getting to Alicia. 'Look at the stars.'

Yes, look at them. It was a cloudless night and even allowing for the lights of the city, the dusty white slash of the Milky Way stood out. 'So many,' I said, more to myself, really.

'Where's the Southern Cross? I can never find it.'

I spotted it almost instantly. 'There, in line with the top of that tree in your neighbour's yard. See the pointers?' I straightened my arm and let it angle over her face.

'Oh, er . . . yeah.' She hadn't actually found it, but didn't want to make a fuss.

'They go forever, the stars,' I said to her. 'Stretched out over billions and billions of kilometres. There's so much of the universe, it's impossible to imagine. Seems like a lot of trouble to go to.'

'What are you talking about, Josh. A lot of trouble!' Alicia flipped over onto her stomach, her body making a watery ripping sound as her skin peeled away from the tiles. 'I'll tell you why there are so many stars. So that lovers can lie back and stare up at them, that's why.' She shifted forward with her elbows until her head was above mine, kissing me playfully. Then she rolled off the edge of the pool into the water.

That was a come-on, but I lingered for a second or two. The stars were still there, far too many of them to make sense. I wanted to talk more about them but Alicia was a dolphin again, the light from the house glistening silver and gold on the fabulous curves of her hips as she arched out of the water and slipped effortlessly under again. I went after her, caught her, let her go and caught her again.

'You sounded a bit disappointed when I rang tonight,' she called from across the pool when I let her escape my lazy grasp. She was teasing me, knowing that I would deny it.

'I thought it might have been Michael.'

'Who's he?'

'My brother.'

'I didn't think you had a brother, just you and Hayley.'

I don't talk about Michael much so it's not surprising that she hadn't heard his name. 'Michael's five years older than me. He hasn't rung home for a few months now so we've been waiting for a call. When he does ring, it's usually at six-thirty, you see. Teatime.'

'So that he can catch your parents?'

'No, that's just it. So that he can talk to me. If Mum or Dad pick up the phone, he just hangs up.'

'Sounds weird.'

'Yeah, I suppose it does. None of us have seen Michael for more than two years. Whenever he rings, there are STD pips at the start so he must be calling from outside Sydney. We don't know where. He won't tell us.'

Alicia had stopped moving away from me and stood still in the water. Must be a hard thing for her to understand. Her family seemed pretty close to one another.

I tried to explain. 'Michael was pretty wild.'

'You're pretty wild yourself, especially your hands,' she replied immediately and there was no need for an explanation after that because I was after her again. She took the safe option and climbed out of the pool before I could catch her.

Dad's Statesman pulled up outside just before ten. Funny how two things get fused together in your mind. For me, the new-car smell of leather upholstery immediately conjures up the sickening stench of vomit. It's because of my brother, Michael. He nearly died in one of Dad's brand new cars.

I was only eleven at the time. Hayley was in hospital because she had broken her arm falling off a swing. We went to visit her in the afternoon, leaving Michael behind to watch a footy game on the TV with one of his mates. It was after dark by the time the nurses asked us to leave. When we got home there was Michael flat out on the carpet of the lounge room with his mate kneeling over him, shaking him, trying to wake him up. Dad was down beside him in a flash, but Michael didn't stir, even when Dad pushed back his eyelids and felt his pulse.

I can still hear the fury in Dad's voice. 'What have you two been up to?'

'Nothing, nothing,' said the friend, but there were empty bottles on the coffee table and on the floor, little brown stubbies mostly, except for the Bundaberg Rum Dad was given by a client the Christmas before.

'This wasn't even open,' he said, glaring at Michael's friend.

'I didn't drink any of it. I stayed on the beer. He was the one,' he said, pointing at Michael on the floor.

'A whole bottle! How many beers did he have beforehand?'

'I don't know,' said the friend, but Mum had checked the kitchen. 'Half a dozen at least, Phil,' she called.

Dad stood over Michael, the fear in his face spreading out into the room, taking hold of all of us. 'We'd better take him to the hospital.' He called Mum to take Michael's legs and together they got him into the back seat of the car. There was no room for me so I sat on Mum's lap in the front with the seat belt over both of us.

We'd only gone a few streets when Michael vomited. Straightaway a gagging noise started up and his chest began to jerk up and down. Dad stopped the car and by the time he was into the back seat with Michael, Mum was shouting. 'He can't breathe, he's choking.'

There was vomit all over Dad's pants, brown and putrid. I wanted to puke myself. Mum was going berserk, 'Don't let him die, Phil, don't let him die,' and I was crying along with her.

'We have to keep going, to the hospital,' Dad called. 'Carol, you'll have to drive.'

Mum didn't want to, but she didn't have a choice. We took off before Dad even had a chance to close the back door. At a red light, Dad yelled at her to go through it and she cried back like he had hit her, but the car kept going. And all the time in the back seat, Michael wasn't breathing. I turned right around, watching the whole thing in horror and crying like a baby because I was so scared.

Dad wrestled Michael's body around and made him sit up in an L shape, then he reached both his arms around my brother's chest, locked his hands together and jerked his arms tight, hard enough to break my brother in half, but instead, some stuff shot out of Michael's mouth so fast it splattered against the window.

'He's still not breathing.' Dad put his ear down onto Michael chest. 'Heart's stopped!'

Mum pulled the car over but Dad screamed at her. 'No, no, keep going for God's sake!'

'I can't.' She was sobbing.

'He'll die unless you keep going!'

I wanted to die. The life was draining out of my brother on the back seat behind me and my parents had gone crazy, yelling at each other like they never had before. Whimpering noises came out of me but with so much other noise, no one heard.

Mum started the car moving while, in the back, Dad was contorting his body again. I peered over the head rest and saw Dad put his mouth over Michael's. It was all crusted with vomit. After a couple of goes, he stopped and pushed himself up high over Michael's chest, pressing down hard with the heels of his hands. He kept swapping between the two, the breathing and pumping Michael's heart and all the time telling Mum to go faster. Then came a sound I can still hear sharp in my ears, the sound of air dragged into desperate lungs.

'He's breathing, Carol, he's breathing.'

Mum pulled into the hospital soon after, driving straight up to the brightly lit Emergency Bay. Dad was out of the back seat before the car had even stopped, covered in Michael's vomit and shouting for the nurses to come out and help him.

They put Michael on a trolley and rolled him away. Not even Dad was allowed to go with him. We all had to wait in the corridor, Mum crying like a river and a nurse trying to comfort her, saying, 'I'm sure he'll be all right. Once they stabilise his condition . . .'

But people get a look on their face when they know everything is fine, a complacent smugness that they already know the danger has passed. It wasn't there on that nurse's face. Dad sat on the other side of Mum, massaging the back of her neck and whispering to her.

I stood against the wall, on my own. The crying had stopped but my whole body was shaking and shivering as though an Arctic winter had set in. Oh God, let Michael be all right. That was the only thought in my mind.

At last a door opened along the corridor. Echoing footsteps became a doctor advancing towards us. 'He's going to make it,' he called when he saw us. 'His lungs are clear and he's breathing on his own again. His heartbeat has stabilised, too. There's no sign of brain damage, though it's just as well you got him breathing again when you did. You'd have lost him, otherwise. They are pumping his stomach now to make sure he doesn't absorb any more alcohol.'

He stepped closer to put his arm over Dad's shoulder, in a

gesture of reassurance, but when he was close enough to smell Dad he stood back. Mum started hugging the nurse. I needed the same comfort and went straight for her, weeping again at the sight of my mother's relief.

But now that all the good news had been delivered, Dad backed away and rested against the wall of the corridor. He crossed his arms over his chest and took hold of his elbows and turned away to press his forehead against the wall. The grimace on his face was like someone had just shoved a knife into his ribs. 'Michael, Michael,' was all he could say, a hoarse and wretched gasp that I don't think he even knew he was making.

Then, for a few seconds until he took control of himself again, my father began to weep in painful, silent sobs. It's the only time I ever saw him like that, the time when Michael nearly died.

chapter four

By Thursday, the journey to the Lost Property Office had become routine. Boarding at Oatley along with the rest of the commuters then on through the St George heartland and in to Central. As he had done on the previous three mornings, Clive arrived exactly two minutes before nine and we opened for business on the dot at nine o'clock.

The thing about Clive Staples is that you could walk right past him in a crowd and not notice him. Brown splotches dot his old man's skin and his stringy hair is always parted neatly on the side, though late in the day the fringe gets tired and hangs down a bit over his high forehead. About the only feature that makes him unusual is his shoulders. Because he is always pulling his head down into them, they seem permanently hunched and too wide for his body. The huge, bi-focal lenses in his glasses are almost square and the frames so old most of the gold paint has flaked off, leaving green patches where his salty sweat has corroded the metal.

Once through the security door and into the blue-walled, blue-carpeted office, I took a closer look at him while he removed a plastic lunch box and thermos from his ancient backpack. Short, leathery fingers, flappy ears like an elephant. Yesterday, as that woman was telling us about her grandmother's brooch, it was his face that had intrigued me. His lips were rather narrow and that doesn't usually make a face very appealing, but when he smiles, he keeps those lips together, pushing the corners way out across his face so that his cheeks swell up. He could be one of Snow White's dwarves.

'Does your wife make those sandwiches for you?'

'She used to, before she died.'

Great question, Josh, especially when I'd only said it as a tease.

'I'm sorry, I didn't mean to . . .'

'That's all right, you weren't to know. Kathleen died ten years ago, from an asthma attack. She was never good about taking her medication,' he added in a wistful tone. 'I still hear her dry cough in the hallway.'

'You stayed in the same house, then?' I was thinking of Mum's sister, Joanne. When she died eighteen months ago her husband sold up straight away; said he couldn't bear all the familiar things they'd shared so close around him.

'Yes, the same house. It's in Strathfield,' Clive was saying. 'We bought it the same year we got married. It's worth too much now.'

'Too much!'

He pushed the thermos into the centre of the table where

it would remain all day. The sandwiches were already in our little bar-fridge beside the safe. 'Bloody real estate agents pester me night and day, ringing me up, asking why don't I want to sell? It's the top of the market. I'll get so much for it. They're trying to lever me out of the place, like an old barnacle.'

No one was going to shove Clive out of Strathfield, that was pretty clear.

'What are you going to do with the money you earn from this job?' he asked in return.

'New speakers for my band.' This needed some explanation and though he listened politely, he wasn't really interested. We hadn't had much to say to each other on the first few days but that woman yesterday had changed things. I wanted to ask him about her; the trouble was, I couldn't quite work out what I wanted to know.

Once I'd mastered the proper procedure for queries and returns, Clive started to leave me alone behind the counter and go downstairs to where the long-term lost property was kept. After smoko on that Thursday, he had a surprise for me.

'I need your expertise for a bit.'

My expertise! What did that mean? He clipped a sign into place behind the perspex screen that said, *Back in Ten Minutes* and off we went, first onto the wide concourse that looked out to the inter-city platforms and then into the sunshine where the taxis lined up for passengers and finally down the ramp into Pitt Street. Here he used a security code to open heavy, dark-green doors and ushered me into a high-ceilinged room about the size of a basketball court.

Not that there was room to bounce a ball in this place. Every centimetre of wall space, even across the filthy and forgotten windows, was taken up by shelving and every centimetre of shelving was crammed with lost property. Trestle tables were set out in rows across the floor, leaving only narrow aisles between them, and they groaned under the weight of even more items. There were handbags, backpacks, briefcases, school bags, dozens of sleeping bags, gameboys, a backgammon set, a broken clarinet and a flute lying neatly in three pieces inside the blue velvet lining of its carry-case. And the clothes! Jumpers, tracksuit tops, running shoes, coats and jackets, baseball caps.

'I'm getting all this ready for the auction in January,' said Clive. 'Most of it is sold, usually.'

'What, all those umbrellas? How will you sell that many?' They covered two tables, six and seven deep.

'Easiest sale of the day. The same bloke comes to every auction and buys the lot. He has a contact in Fiji. Rains every day in Fiji. Did you know that, Josh? Makes for a roaring trade in second-hand umbrellas.'

Clive was marching purposefully along one of the aisles but I was still stuck by the door, trying to take it all in. Everything in this room had been lost by someone, left behind, misplaced, forgotten about until it was too late. My eye caught something odd in the corner – arms and legs, a large plastic bin full of them.

'Oh, gross, what's this lot, Clive!'

He turned to look. 'Prosthetic limbs. They're the one thing we don't sell. Have to keep them here, by law.'

Some were straight and some were bent at right angles, as though a Hindu God had been stuffed headfirst into a snake charmer's basket. 'How can anyone leave an artificial leg behind?' I picked one up, surprised by its weight. 'What did the guy do, hop? Surely he would have noticed.'

'Apparently not,' Clive said wryly. He had arrived at where he wanted to be and waited patiently for me to join him. 'There's no point auctioning this stuff individually. A lot of the bidders run flea-market stalls and second-hand shops. They're looking for bargains in bulk and that's why I brought you down here, Josh. You know a bit about pop music, don't you?'

Pop music! Gimme a break.

My disdain went unnoticed. 'See this pile of CDs,' he said, nodding down at the bench top. 'It's young people's music mostly. I haven't got much of a clue, to be honest. Maurie usually sorts it out, but he's off on his honeymoon. Could you sort them into bundles of five according to what goes with what?'

'Sure,' I answered, mildly chuffed that he'd asked me. There was some decent stuff, too, albums I'd love to have myself. 'How much do these CDs sell for?'

'Oh, twenty dollars for five, some of them. The dealers don't like to pay much more.'

'Twenty bucks. Hey, I might end up at this auction myself. When did you say it was?'

'First Saturday after New Year,' he answered, leaving me to it. 'Make sure you slam this door hard before you come back upstairs.'

I stacked the CDs roughly into hip-hop, heavy metal,

pop-princess or whatever and began to make up the bundles. It was harder than you'd expect but as my hands shuffled and reshuffled, I picked out the five that appealed most to me, five that, just coincidentally, weren't yet part of my collection.

Fifteen minutes and it was done. I slammed the door as instructed and headed back the way I'd come. Clive was serving a customer at the counter when I arrived.

'Look, I'll recognise it once I see it,' said the customer. Even with his back to me, I could tell the guy wasn't very happy with Clive. 'It's a Canon digital, right. Why don't you just show me the ones that have been handed in.'

'That's not the way we work, sir,' Clive said calmly from behind the screen. 'Could I see some identification, please, and some proof of purchase?'

'What's that?'

'A receipt from the store where you bought the camera. If it's so new, I'm sure you will still have it, for warranty purposes.'

'I'm not here to talk about any warranty. I want my camera.'

'Sir, we can't let you have anything unless you show some ID and clear evidence that it is yours.'

The guy backed away a step and started to complain loudly. 'You're cheating me. Where's your manager? I'll go to the papers about this,' but he was retreating even further, past me and halfway up the ramp. Then he was gone altogether.

I let myself in through the security door. 'What was all that about?'

Clive sighed. 'It's the ad in the paper,' he said, but when he saw that I didn't have a clue, he explained, 'Happens every year, with cameras especially. The newspaper advertisements for the auction always make a big thing out of the cameras and opportunists like that bloke can't resist. Why bid at the auction if he can come here first and claim one as his own? With a bit of bluff and bravado he's got something he can sell out the side door of a pub for a hundred dollars and it hasn't cost him a cent.'

This story was fresh in my ears when I came back from lunch at the kiosk. A man followed me tentatively down the ramp and since Clive was still sipping his tea I went straight to the counter.

'Hi,' I called to the figure now waiting on the other side of the perspex.

The guy jumped as though my greeting had jabbed him in the ribs. That first response put me on my guard and now that I took a close look at him, this new customer was definitely dodgy. Lank, greasy hair slapped in rats' tails at his shoulders and three days of dark fuzz hid his hollow cheeks and chin, but the give-away was his moistened eyes that looked everywhere except straight at me.

'I'm looking . . . I'm trying to find something . . . I've come to see about something I left on a train.'

Right, I'll do everything by the book with this guy. A stab at the space bar brought the computer screen to life with a query page all ready to be filled in. 'What did you lose?'

'A bag.'

'What sort of bag?'

'It was . . . like a small backpack,' he said, making anxious movements with his hands, trying to show me the size.

'What was inside it?'

'A book, a diary but with room for addresses and phone numbers at the back,' he answered immediately.

A diary! The guy must be genuine after all, but just as I started to relax, he added, 'And a camera.'

Back on the alert. 'When did you leave it on the train?'

This time he paused for a long time and my suspicions flicked well into the red. 'Five months ago,' he told me finally.

'Five months! Why has it taken you so long to come looking for this bag?'

He closed his eyes and swayed for a moment. 'I'd rather not say.'

And I would rather not hand anything over to this bloke, either. 'Can you remember what train you were travelling on when you left the bag behind?'

'Down to Wollongong. I was going to get off at Thirroul.' He sounded certain about the destination, but there was something in the way he said he'd been 'going to'. 'Did you get off at Thirroul then, sir?'

His eyes were on the move again and from his body language you would think I was threatening to punch him in the stomach. 'No, that was why I lost the bag. I was . . . at least, I had to get off earlier.'

I didn't even sense Clive close by until he spoke from behind me.

'What colour was the backpack?'

'Blue, light blue.'

'Do you remember the brand?'

'No, I'm sorry. I never took any notice. It was a cheap one I bought at an op-shop. The only way to identify it would be from the diary and from the camera, too.'

Back to the camera. He always mentioned it second, as though we wouldn't notice. Clive seemed to accept the man's story entirely, though there was something in his voice – a touch of regret, even sadness.

'A light-blue backpack, with a camera and a diary, on the Wollongong line, five months ago?' said Clive who had obviously been listening longer than a few seconds.

The man at the counter thought for a second. 'It might be closer to six months.'

'I'll go and check for you, sir,' said Clive.

What was he doing? Hadn't he heard the guy? It was at least five months ago, maybe six. The backpack would have been taken downstairs ages ago. 'We normally don't keep items up here for longer than two months,' I warned.

Clive had disappeared around the corner by this time, leaving me with the customer who looked as though my last words had been a death sentence. He didn't want to believe me, obviously, because he craned his neck to see where Clive had gone. The deep and gentle booms of the compactus told me Clive was rolling shelf after shelf along the rails.

I went behind the screen to have a look and found Clive in the last bay, hauling an old suitcase from behind the folded-up prams and strollers. He seemed annoyed that I had followed him. 'Go back to the counter, Josh,' he ordered.

I went, but when Clive returned, there was no sign of the suitcase. He wasn't carrying anything at all, but if his hands were empty, his face certainly wasn't. Those narrow lips were turned down at each end and his melancholy expression wouldn't have been out of place on a beagle. 'I'm sorry, sir, there is no light-blue bag from so long ago and no diary either. It's the diary you're after, isn't it?'

The customer nodded and closed his eyes again briefly. His hands slipped to the edge of the counter and he had to grip it hard to steady himself. Any second, he was going to burst into tears and the thought sent my mind back to the woman with the missing brooch.

But we simply didn't have what this guy was looking for and there wasn't much point in him hanging around, staring at us. He seemed to realise this himself and turned until Clive called to him. 'I'm sorry we don't have it, but it was never handed in to us here. It meant a great deal to you, didn't it.'

'Irreplaceable,' the man whispered. It wasn't at all the kind of word I expected from someone so dishevelled and unsure of himself.

'The diary may be gone, but not the people you wrote in it,' said Clive. 'There are other ways to contact them.'

'No, you don't understand. I can't remember. You see, the

treatment. . . .' He didn't finish, but frowned so deeply and swallowed so hard that his entire face seemed to cave in.

'Would you like to come in and sit down for a minute?' Clive asked.

'No, no, I'm all right,' the man said hastily, holding up his hands as though Clive was trying to touch him. Then he dropped them and stared into Clive's face with such intensity that I had to have a look myself. They made a good pair. If I didn't know better, I would have guessed Clive was the one who had lost the diary and all the people it connected him to.

'Thank you,' said the man and though he still looked downcast, he seemed to have accepted the disappointment without the risk of falling to pieces that had hung around him until now.

Clive went back to the table and poured himself another cup of tea from the thermos. I followed him and sat down in the second chair. 'You really wanted to find that diary, didn't you?'

'It was important to him.'

'Like the brooch.'

'Yes, like the brooch.' Clive took a sip from the white plastic cup.

An odd question rolled off my tongue before I could stop it. 'You care, don't you, Clive?'

'Care about what?' he asked before he had quite swallowed the mouthful.

'About that guy just now and the woman yesterday.'

He shrugged and didn't deny it.

'Why? Why did those two matter so much to you? There are people coming to the counter all the time.'

'Some are special,' he said, leaning back in his chair, his eyes fixed on the thermos in front of him.

'What, so special that you invite them in for a cup of tea?'

Clive hesitated, slowly lifting his head to let his grey eyes rest on me. 'Couldn't you see how much that bloke needed his diary, Josh?'

'He looked a bit nuts to me. Why would he leave it so long to come looking for the bag? If that address book was so precious to him he should have rung up the next day. And how could he forget so much? The addresses and phone numbers, sure, I can believe that, but people's names!'

Clive looked down at his cup and didn't answer, leaving me feeling stupid and wishing that I hadn't asked him why he cared. I thought again about the joy in that woman's face when Clive brought out her brooch. Why did that scene stick in my mind so much?

The afternoon dragged by with me at the counter while Clive tagged items in the safe for the auction. Cameras mostly. That set me wondering. Why hadn't Clive done a computer search for the sad guy's camera? If we had it after all, the camera would still be in the safe. Instead, he'd headed back into the compactus. And what about that suitcase? Suitcases belonged in Bay Three, not down the end amongst the baby capsules and fold-up prams.

chapter five

Every year my Dad's family gets together for the Tambling Christmas party. Because Aunty Erica lives in Newcastle and most families want to stay at home on Christmas Day anyway, the party is held on the Sunday before. This year it was at Aunty Denise's. She's got a pool and plenty of space for my cousins to muck about in; just as well because there are a million of them. Denise has four kids plus a husband, Warren (Big Wazza), who is a bit like an extra kid; then there is Leonie with her four; Erica who has two and another one due in February and finally Uncle Bernie who hasn't started yet, although he's been living with Clare for three years.

Plus Grandma. Grandma Tambling is seventy-five and on days like the Christmas get-together, the smile never leaves her face. There is no Grandad Tambling. He died when I was three and no one talks about him much.

As soon as we arrived, Big Wazza stuck a cold stubby in Dad's hand. 'Get that inside ya, and there's plenty more in the esky.'

'Great, thanks,' said Dad but this was the start of an annual pantomime. Half an hour later, Wazza called, 'Ready for another, Phil?'

Dad held up his stubby holder. 'Still going on this one, Warren.'

By lunchtime his answer switched to, 'Oh, better be careful. Have to drive home, don't I.' Big Wazza never managed to get more than one beer into my father.

In fact, *not* drinking earned Dad a picture on the front page of the *Sydney Morning Herald*. It was taken the day after the Grand Final and shows him at the wheel of a bus with a dozen legless footballers behind him all waving their beer cans at the camera. The caption made a big thing out of Dad because all he'd had to drink was a mouthful of champagne from the trophy and so he was sober enough to drive the bus on their victory tour around the suburbs.

That picture is in one of the scrapbooks Grandma put together. 'The best footballer never to play for Australia'; that's what they say about Phil Tambling. I used to pore over those scrapbooks, so proud that it was my father who had all those articles written about him in *Rugby League Week* and the *Telegraph* and the *Sydney Morning Herald*.

When Uncle Bernie and Clare finally turned up, we gathered around the Christmas tree. Grandma played Santa Claus with help from Big Wazza who slipped onto his knees beside her and handed up the presents one by one.

'Here's yours, Josh,' called Grandma, demanding a kiss on the cheek before she would part with the thin square, wrapped neatly in red and green paper. CD, of course. Aunt Erica was watching me open it.

'Bone Jar,' I said in mock surprise but I already knew it would be their live gig at Georgia Tech because Erica had called Mum and Mum had asked me. If she'd ignored the advice and chosen some other gift, I was going to buy the CD next week anyway.

Without wanting to put a dampener on the fun, that set me wondering whether there was any Christmas present that I couldn't buy for myself with what I was earning at the Lost Property Office. A trip to see an Oasis concert in London, a red Monaro coupé, maybe, but that was wishlist stuff, pure fantasy, like those lotto ads on TV, and so they didn't count.

Standing there, watching the wrapping paper come off, nothing came to mind. It sounds crazy, but I've got just about everything I want and when new things come up I can always get hold of them or Mum and Dad'll buy them for me, like my Fender. That was pretty much Gemma's point from the other night, and it made me squirm, remembering. Made me think ahead to tonight as well, when the guys and I were jamming again. Would Gemma be there?

A squeal brought my head back into Aunty Denise's lounge room where Grandma was giving out extra presents to my younger cousins. One of them had scored a Harry Potter outfit, complete with wand, round glasses and a stick-on lightning bolt for his forehead. Now there was a happy kid.

That was me, once. It wasn't a Harry Potter outfit though, but a Roman soldier's kit – the best thing: a sword, a shield, a helmet and a breastplate, all made of cheap grey plastic. I was a centurion for weeks afterwards.

My little cousins went on opening presents, their faces filled with the same excitement the soldier's outfit had brought me, back when I was seven, or eight, or whatever. It was like the joy I'd seen in that woman when Clive found her brooch. Was that why I had sat in the train on the way home, unable to get her out of my mind? Was it envy? Did I just want to feel happy like these little kids with their cheap Christmas presents?

At Steve's place later that night, Gemma appeared before we had even made a start. She was better dressed this time in a strappy top that made the best of her slender neck and shoulders. There were even touches of make-up around her eyes and her mouth but best of all, those delicate feet were still bare.

'What, no party to go to?' said Neven to stir her up.

'Not many boys have improved since Year Six,' she came back at him, as though it was still Wednesday night. 'I've given up on them,' she continued, but as she spoke she transferred her flirty smirk to me and said, 'Well most of them, anyway.'

Hey, eat my dust, Neven!

Then the deliberate provocation gave way to a laugh, as though she couldn't keep up the performance any longer. Neven sent me a confused glance. She had his measure, all right. In return, I nodded towards her naked feet and did the thing with my eyebrows.

That was enough for Neven. 'Come on, Dave, get that bloody bass plugged in,' he snapped. 'We'll start with *Cheated*.'

It's a Bluntblade song, loud and none too happy with the world but it wasn't the wildest headbanger in our play-list. There's a stretch in the middle where I stop singing and let Neven take over with a long lead break he's been working on. Bloody show off!

Halfway through his star turn, Gemma started dancing enthusiastically in front of him, moving her head and stretching her arms out for balance. It was like having a mosh pit of one and I couldn't wait until the vocals kicked in again so she would connect with me instead.

But when the moment came I found myself wrenching out a tragic cry of someone driven only by frustration and despair.

Why do you love when no heart can feel you?
Give all you've got then someone will steal you.
The world turns it back, you might as well die,
They took all the earth, now they want the sky.

The mood that we'd built up through the instrumental break died instantly and Gemma stopped dancing altogether. Cheated! Yeah, that's just how I felt, adding a strange authenticity to the rage I was supposed to be expressing through the words. When the song ended, its anger stayed in me and the whole thing left me flat instead of feeling purged and exhilarated.

Gemma went straight over to Neven. The pair of them had their backs to me while he replayed riffs from his lead break and she swayed beside him, unconsciously recalling how she had moved her hips so enticingly. After that first song though, there wasn't much for Gemma to dance along with and she soon left us.

It was one of those breathless, humid nights when the heat lingers long after the sun has gone down. And if the air was tropical outside, the atmosphere was downright sweltering in the garage.

After an hour, we couldn't stand it any more. By then our shirts were off and grimy rivers of sweat trickled down our chests, our stomachs, our backs.

'Open the doors, let some air in,' Neven demanded.

When Steve raised the roller-door we found Gemma out in the driveway. 'There's a breeze starting up. Come out here and feel it,' she called, waving us towards her.

The night air was cooling down at last and on our hot, dripping skins its breath was better than a swim. We couldn't face the furnace of the garage again and stayed out in the front yard instead, sprawled out on the grass while Gemma perched on an ornamental rock at the edge of the garden, like a life-size gnome. For the second time in just a couple of days, I was on my back and looking up at the stars.

Gemma noticed. 'There's the Southern Cross,' she said, pointing. She had it right, too.

'What about Orion?' I asked.

She found that without any trouble so I asked her a harder one. 'Can you find the Centaur?'

'If you guys are going to play Stars of the Night Sky, I'm going for a drink,' said Steve.

'Yeah, bring us one, too,' Neven demanded lazily.

'Come and get it yourself.'

Dave didn't bother to ask, but simply got to his feet and trailed after them, his size thirteens shuffling like a sleep-walker.

All this happened without really breaking the conversation between Gemma and me. 'Do you know how far away those stars are?' I asked her.

'They measure it in light years, don't they?'

'Yeah, the numbers would be too large otherwise. Even the closest star is four light-years away. That's twenty-five thousand trillion kilometres or something. Worked it out once, just for the hell of it. And there are galaxies up there billions of light-years away. It doesn't make sense.'

'What do you mean, it doesn't make sense?'

'It's all a monumental waste,' I said, aware that I'd started to say these things to Alicia.

There was no pool for Gemma to roll into like there had been for Alicia and she seemed to understand that these stats weren't just rattled off to sound clever.

'That's a weird thing to say, Josh. How can it be a waste? The stars are just there, part of the universe.'

'But why is it so big? I mean, we haven't even worked out how big the universe is yet. It's mind-boggling just trying to imagine and most of it's so far away we'll never reach it.'

'Does that matter? We've got our own little part of it. That's all we need.'

'Exactly. That's all we need, so why go to all the fuss of making the rest?'

Gemma laughed, more of a sniff really. 'Don't ask me. You need a higher authority to answer that one.' She flicked her eyes upward, eyebrows too, but left the word 'God' unsaid.

'Another waste of time,' I muttered.

Gemma had been sitting back, resting on her hands with her head tilted to the night sky, but now she leaned forward to look straight down at me. 'Sounds like you don't believe there is a such a thing.'

Had I sounded like that? Words are dangerous. They can give you away if you're not careful. The seconds ticked on, waiting for the silence to be filled by my answer. A quick chuckle would be enough and then the world would move on just that tiny bit with no answer from me at all. But I was tired of that and for once the truth escaped. 'No, I don't.'

Gemma's eyebrows twitched and I wondered whether it was my words that had surprised her, or my unguarded honesty. She was going to say something but before she could speak, the guys made a noisy return. What had she been going to say?

Neven was the last to emerge through the Kominsky's front door. He carried two glasses, the ice clinking invitingly in each. Great, he's brought one for me, I thought until he handed the second glass to Gemma who made space on her rock for him to sit beside her.

chapter six

God is not something you talk about, certainly not to mates like Dave and Neven. Gemma was the first person I'd ever told. The only person.

That was three nights ago. Now it was Christmas Eve, a tick past eight o'clock and the Tambling family was in church for the Vigil Mass, with Mum next to the side aisle, then Hayley and me beside her, and finally Dad who was watching the priest come down the centre. It was always this way, Mum on one end and Dad on the other, a pair of bookends.

It was hard to say how I made the big decision; thinking and reading, mostly. It's not like Fidelis College has any books in the library about how *not* to believe in God, but they have plenty on the universe and biology and different cultures. I've borrowed a few for assignments in Study of Religion, books about Islam, the Jews, Buddhism, but none of them had an answer for the question that'd started to niggle at me. How do we know it's all true?

Stupid question, really, because we can't. The whole point is that you are supposed to have faith, and there was the problem for me. I began to suspect a monumental con job. That was about the middle of this year and every Sunday since then, every Study of Religion period, every time we started or finished the school day with a prayer, I worked out a little more of what was wrong. Wasn't long before my belief in the whole set up had cracked wide open.

Take the stars and galaxies that I talked about with Gemma. What a piece of overkill. This all-powerful God wants to create a world for his beloved human beings, but instead of a few stars and planets spread out over a distance that would give us all plenty of room to play and explore, he puts most of the Universe far out of our reach. Why bother, if he was going to remain so obsessed with just one species that he came down to live on our planet?

This led me to the question that *can* have an answer. Is the universe the way it is because God made it that way, or simply because it happened that way? Over those weeks and months, I started to look for a different answer. What I'd been taught didn't make any sense. It made far more sense to accept that no intelligent force had anything to do with it at all – that it just happened.

Gradually, a lot of other things seemed to fall into place, like why Mum's sister, Joanne, died last year when she had three kids who needed her and a whole parish praying their hearts out. Was it because God decided to leave all those prayers unanswered or because he simply wasn't there to listen in the first place?

No, God is all in our minds. Or at least he's in the minds of the people around me, but he's not in mine, not any more.

It's easy to say those things in my head. No one hears but me, and certainly not my father, standing beside me. He was paying attention to the mass, doing his best to listen to the earnest waffle of the priest who was working his way through a homily about the meaning of Christmas. Later, when we are on our knees, Dad will drop his eyes to the floor for a few moments and pray silently, a personal plea to God about Michael, most likely. Please, Lord, send Michael home to us and keep him safe.

I want to say, there's no one listening, Dad. If Michael is okay it is more because of luck and if he ever comes home it will be because he's desperate and needs help.

Wish I had Michael's balls when it came to all this. 'I'm not going,' he shouted through his bedroom door one Sunday morning when Dad called us all to get ready for church.

'We're a family and we all go,' Dad told him.

'Not me. I'm staying in bed. It's all a load of boring bullshit anyway and I'm sick of it.'

They argued, but in the end, short of dragging Michael down to the church in his pyjamas, there was nothing Dad could do about it. That was when my brother was sixteen, a year younger than I am now.

I remember the disappointment in Dad's face, though, and that's the trouble. I don't want to make him look like that again. The whole religion thing means a lot to Dad, even if he doesn't talk about it much.

So I keep going to church along with the rest of the family. It's not very honest and I hate that, hate myself, hate the whole situation, but I just can't do it. I can't disappoint Dad like Michael did, can't tell him that I don't believe any more.

There were still presents under our own tree on Christmas morning – my present to Mum, to Dad, to Hayley, hers to me and the rest. I scored a new pair of Stüssy shorts and an upgrade kit for my computer. I could've had a mobile but I needed the upgrade for my MP3 files. Once the wrapping paper was cleared away, Dad went off in the Statesman to get Grandma and by the time he returned, Mum's brother-in-law, Brad, had arrived with my three motherless cousins.

After lunch we moved out to the pool where the adults lay back in banana lounges moaning, 'I feel like a python. I won't have to eat for a month. Why did you let me eat so much?'

My cousins wanted to play Crocodile Attack so I was underwater when the phone rang, surfacing to find Mum calling frantically over the pool fence. I was still dripping wet when she handed me the phone. 'We think it's him. A voice asked for you and hasn't said anything else.'

'Hello?'

'Josh, mate. Merry Christmas. How the bloody hell are you?'

It was Michael all right.

'I'm fine. Happy Christmas to you.' It was hard to concentrate with Mum's eyes on me, and Dad's and Grandma's and even the kids who had gone quiet in that way when something adult and serious has killed their game.

'Are . . . are you okay yourself, Michael?' I asked.

'Bloody great. I'm doing real well, in fact, Josh. You wouldn't believe it.'

Yes, that was just it. You couldn't always believe Michael. Doing all right to him might mean he hadn't had a run in with the cops for a few weeks.

'Where are you living?' I asked.

'Ah, now, Josh, you know better than to ask me that. I'm living in a nice spot, a paradise, you might say. Plenty of people would swap with me, if they had the chance.'

Could the tone of his voice tell me anything? There had been calls in the past when he sounded dispirited and achingly lonely, but he wasn't like that this time. Maybe he had been celebrating Christmas Day in a pub.

'Are you coming home soon?'

'No, I'm not coming home, Josh. I've told you that before and you can tell Mum and Dad, too. Tell them I'm doing okay and they don't need to worry about me.'

Fat chance of that. They worried all the time. 'Do you want to speak to them? Mum's right here beside me.'

I shouldn't have suggested it. Michael wasn't likely to agree, anyway, but we'll never know because Mum wrenched the phone out of my hand. 'Michael, Michael, where are you? Why won't you speak to your father and me and let us know where you are. It's not fair . . .' She didn't say any more because the line had gone dead.

Mum stood staring down at the lifeless phone in her hand. Without a human sound to cut across them, the cicadas had the backyard to themselves and on such a hot, sunny day they weren't wasting the opportunity. Their steady note made the human silence more unbearable.

Then Mum was crying, great wrenching sobs that racked her body and threw her off balance. Dad was beside her in a flash, putting his arm around her shoulders and trying to draw her in close to him. But Mum wouldn't have it. With an awkward, angry twist of her body, she broke free and pushed his arm away so hard he almost spun round. Her face was screwed into that wild and desperate glare you see on kids in the school-yard when they've been teased so much they're ready to lash out. But the moment passed and instead of attacking, Mum bolted into the house, leaving Dad embarrassed and bewildered among the rest of us. A few moments later, he went after her.

Uncle Brad tried to get Hayley and me back into the pool with his kids, but the tension was too much and we huddled beside Grandma, listening to the noises coming from the house. Mum wasn't crying now, she was shouting.

'You drove him away, you threw him out like a sack of garbage. No wonder he doesn't want to have anything to do with us. You should never have treated him like that.'

Dad's not a shouter. He gets angry all right and when he does I'm afraid to look in his eyes, but I've never heard him rant like Mum was doing. There was no chance of the afternoon going on as usual after that. Uncle Brad had a word in

Grandma's ear and with a solemn nod of the head between them, he called to his kids. 'Get your things. We have to go.'

I carried a bag of damp towels out to their car and waved them off, then returned to the pool. Grandma was stacking plates though her mind really wasn't on the job. Hayley looked anxiously towards the house.

'What's going on, Josh? I've never seen Mum like this before.'

'It's the way Michael rings and won't talk to her.'

Hayley made a face, obviously unsatisfied with my answer.

'Your Mum worries about him in a special way,' said Grandma, who had abandoned the dishes and come to stand beside us. 'She loves you two just as much, don't ever doubt that, but Michael was her first and they didn't have an easy time of it, the pair of them.'

This was new. I thought I'd heard all the family stories a hundred times.

'What happened?' Hayley asked.

Grandma's wince showed her reluctance to say any more. Maybe Hayley was too young to hear it, or was I the wrong sex? 'There were complications. Your brother was in too much of a hurry to be born. He spent the first six weeks of his life in hospital. That's a hard thing for a new mother. Poor Carol,' she added under her breath while her eyes darted back to the house. Another cry from inside stopped any more questions we might have asked. We couldn't make out the words this time, just Mum's tormented voice.

'I might go inside, see if I can help,' said Grandma. After a few tentative steps she turned back to us. 'You two stay here. I'll come for you when the time is right.'

Hayley started to shiver. It was thirty-five degrees and she was shaking like a leaf, her athlete's body reverting to a little girl's. There wasn't much I could do except wrap a dry towel around her and sit her down among the bowls of chips and the plates dotted with crumbs from the Christmas cake. Flies buzzed in beneath the steady drone of the cicadas and swam in the abandoned glasses of lemonade.

When the shaking stopped, Hayley kept her eyes on the pavers and said softly, 'We sat out here before, do you remember?'

Remember! 'It was Michael shouting that time,' I reminded her.

'I couldn't even tell what he was yelling about,' said Hayley. 'I just remember how angry Dad was and how Mum brought us out here.'

It wasn't surprising that Hayley didn't know what that blow up had been about. She was barely ten years old back then. But I knew. 'Hayles,' I said, 'you know what marijuana is?'

'Oh der, Josh, I'm not a baby,' she shot back at me, sitting up straighter now and letting the towel drop away from her shoulders.

'Well, Michael used to smoke it down in his room.'

She considered this for a few seconds then seemed to make up her mind. 'So what, Sherrie Langdon says her parents smoke it all the time,' and suddenly I felt like a school teacher preaching about the evil of drugs. 'All right, all right, he wasn't the only one,' I replied, dropping the big brother tone from my voice. 'The thing is, he could have smoked all he liked round at his mates' places, but he did it here.'

'On purpose, you mean, like he wanted to make Mum and Dad mad.'

I nodded. Michael didn't even close the door of his bedroom, as though he wanted the sickly sweet smell to drift up the staircase and into the living room.

'It worked, then,' said Hayley matter-of-factly. 'Dad was *so* mad at Michael, but he didn't have to throw him out of the house for that.'

'It wasn't because of the marijuana, and anyway, Dad didn't throw him out, he asked him to leave.'

'Same thing, isn't it?'

How could I explain the difference? I wasn't even sure there was any, but I knew where Hayley had picked up those words from. *Throw him out.* They were Mum's words and Hayley had heard them as clearly as I had. *Thrown out like a sack of garbage.* 'There was more to it than that, Hayles.'

'The police came round, didn't they?'

'Yeah, the police.'

'They told Dad to make Michael go. Is that what happened?'

Again she had the story around the wrong way. 'No, it was Dad who talked the police out of arresting him.' He could do it because of his name, his reputation.

The glare she settled on me said she didn't believe it.

'Look, I was there, Hayley. Michael was pissing himself

down in his room. The cops would've taken him if Dad hadn't talked them out of it. They trusted him to sort Michael out.'

'All I remember is how they argued.'

Our brother had been gone more than two years but Hayley and I had never talked about these things before. No wonder she'd made up her own version of what happened. She didn't know Michael at all, not the way I knew him.

'Yes, they argued, but Michael just hung around the house all the time and bummed off Mum and Dad, took crap jobs and never kept one for more than a few weeks. You didn't see all the times Mum and Dad gave him a second chance, sobered him up after parties, forked out for the damage he caused. It was mostly Michael who started the arguments, anyway. The only time Dad lost it a little was when Michael packed in his apprenticeship.'

'What apprenticeship?' she asked, still wary, but hungry enough for information to listen.

'Carpentry. Michael said it was what he wanted to do so Dad asked around his clients, found him a spot. Then after two weeks, Michael just walked away. Dad was really mad about that.'

'Didn't Michael want to be a builder then?'

'I don't think Michael knew what he wanted. Dad was just angry because he wouldn't stick at it, at least give it a try. Look, I saw it all, Hayles, the way he screwed Mum and Dad tighter and tighter. It was after he chucked in the apprenticeship that he started disappearing for days at a time. Wouldn't tell them where he was until they reported him missing.'

'Why does he do it, Josh?' she asked. 'Why does he only speak to you on the phone?'

It didn't have anything to do with us being brothers, I knew that much. 'It's because they wouldn't give him any money, I think.'

Hayley stared at me, none the wiser.

'You know how he went off to live with his mates at first.'

She nodded uncertainly. It was more than two years ago after all.

'Then sometimes Michael'd be here when we got home from school?'

'He always left before Dad turned up,' Hayley cut in to show she followed me.

'Michael could always twist Mum round his little finger. She'd give him money if he said the right things, that he loved her. She was always a sucker for that line. Then Dad found out and stopped her.'

'Is that when he took off to the Gold Coast?'

'With a couple of guys, yeah. After that, the calls started. I picked up the phone one day and there he was, drunk by the sound of it, swearing and shouting, telling Mum and Dad that he didn't need them, stuff like that. Once he realised it was only me, he sort of laughed and told me to tell them all he'd said, word for word, all the swearing, everything.'

The surface of the pool was a perfect sheet of glass. It's a wonder the vibration from our voices didn't register, like our own seismograph, picking up the slightest tremors. A leaf from the neighbour's gum tree corkscrewed its way to dead-centre, spoiling the perfection. My eyes broke away, towards the house, willing Mum to appear, smiling, waving us inside as though nothing had happened.

'Can't you make him talk to them?' My sister's words were a slap in the face and the anger welled out through my throat before I could stop it. 'It's not my job. I can't make him do the right thing,' but when I saw Hayley cower away I almost cried with regret.

'Hayles,' I said gently, 'do you remember one time on the beach, all of us together, even Michael? He and Dad took turns with a tennis ball, to see who could throw the furthest, and I was the judge?'

I must have been about ten at the time. Every one of us was laughing, at whatever was said, whatever one of us would do – a handstand from Michael, or when I skimmed shells across the waves and most of them sank at the first hit until finally I got one to bounce off the water more times than we could count and everybody clapped. Sometimes I ache to be ten years old again, before that bottle of rum . . . before the arguments . . . before, before, before.

Hayley thought about this for a second then shook her head. 'Not on a beach, not with Michael.'

'Yes, you do.' And it suddenly really mattered to me that she have that memory in her head. 'Afterwards we all went for a long walk, you rode on Dad's shoulders. You were terrified at being so high off the ground but you didn't want to come down either. And Mum said she wished she could stop the sun going down so we could stay on that beach forever and

Michael ran to the top of the dune and stood with his arms above his head so that it looked like he was holding up the sun, keeping it there, like she'd asked.'

It was no use. Hayley frowned at my attempts to jog her memory and then confessed. 'Josh, sometimes I have to think hard just to remember Michael's face.'

After half an hour, Grandma came to take us inside. Mum was sitting on the sofa, tired-eyed and with a guarded smile that mirrored Grandma's, the smoothed-over face that says everything's all right, for now.

'I'm sorry I was so silly,' she said and opened her arms to Hayley who took the bait and rushed to be comforted.

Fine for Hayley but I stood back, doing my best to ignore the brittle edge in my mother's voice, and her shoulders held stiffly in place. Michael's stubborn absence and those phone calls were slowly wearing her away to nothing, but watching her, a new fear crept under my skin, that before this could happen, she would simply break into a dozen tormented pieces and not even Dad could keep her together.

chapter seven

About four, Dad announced he was taking Grandma home.

'Could you go past Alicia's?' I asked. 'It's sort of in that direction.'

He considered the logistics. 'Sure, but if you want me to pick you up again on the way home, you won't be able to stay long.'

'That's fine,' I answered. In fact, it was perfect.

We drove in uncomfortable silence as far as Alicia's house. Her Christmas present was digging into my leg through the pocket of the new Stüssy shorts. I hadn't had a clue what to get her so I'd asked her friend, Melanie Stewart.

'She'd love you to give her a ring.'

'You're just stirring me, right?' There was no way I was giving Alicia a ring.

'No, seriously,' she insisted. 'Just a flea-market one would be fine. Won't cost you much.'

I asked for another suggestion.

'She was looking at silver chains when we were in town last week. A really fine one.'

'Has she bought it yet?'

'Not as far as I know.'

So I'd bought Alicia a silver chain in its own little box lined with tissue paper and asked Hayley to wrap it nicely for me. She'd done a great job, too, tying gold ribbon around the glossy red paper and using the scissor blades to do some-thing to the loose ends that turned them into Goldilocks' curls.

Dad dropped me on the opposite side of the road, calling, 'I'll be by again in fifteen minutes, Josh.'

That would be long enough. When Alicia opened the door she held a finger to her lips. 'They're all sleeping off lunch or watching TV,' she whispered, nodding towards the family room. She was holding one hand behind her back, rather obvi-ously. 'Let's go out to the pool.'

Fine by me. The sun was still high, but not so high that the trees at the bottom of the garden couldn't shade us from the worst of it. Leaves from those same trees crunched under my feet and peppered the pool's surface. Should have brought my board shorts. We sat side by side around a wrought-iron table and finally the present emerged from behind her back, neatly wrapped with the same ribbon and curls that Hayley had done for me. No amount of ribbon could disguise the fact that it was a CD.

'Merry Christmas, Josh,' she said, staring into my eyes.

We hesitated, then leaned forward onto the edge of the table for a kiss – just a Christmas smooch.

'Open it.'

Music is my game, right, so without undoing the bow, I tore away the paper to see what it was. But before I had ripped away half of the wrapping my eyes froze; it was the Bone Jar CD, the one Aunt Erica had given me last Sunday.

'I heard you talking about it,' said Alicia, her eyes shining as they caught a beam of sunlight through the trees.

'Thanks. This is great.' So what if this album had been spinning in my CD player all week? Not the end of the world and no way was I going to spoil Alicia's fun, though that couldn't stop me feeling let down, as if this innocent mix-up summed up the way our relationship was going.

Dad was back a little after four-thirty. He saw the present in my hand. 'Alicia gave you a CD for Christmas, did she?'

'Yeah. Bone Jar.' No need to tell him the whole story. 'It's good. I've been wanting to get it for a while.'

'Anything I'd like?' he asked, without taking his eyes from the road ahead. He expected me to say no, of course – all part of a joke we've got going between us. He absolutely hates the kind of music we play in the band.

'Why does it have to be so loud?' he complained.

Loud! We didn't have the speakers to really let it rip.

'If it's too loud, then you're too old,' I taunted him, quoting Johnny Rotten.

Still, he's pleased that I know my way around a guitar and

he turned up at all the boring concerts at school to see his son in the Guitar Ensemble and all the other crap that makes me cringe these days. And there's the minor fact that he bought me the Fender, so he can diss my music all he likes. In return, I give him heaps about the easy listening shit he listens to in the Statesman.

My eye ran down the list of songs on the Bone Jar album. He'd hate every one. No, wait, I *could* call his bluff after all. Bone Jar's singer, Freddy Riebolt,had covered an old song from the sixties for some movie soundtrack. There it was, *Lovebroke* – words and music by Don Jennings. Dad was always going on about Don Jennings and his group. It was Dad's band, as big as the Beatles, he reckoned, until this Jennings guy drowned in a freak accident.

I slipped the disc into the slot in the middle of the console while Dad watched suspiciously. 'What are you up to?'

Victory would be sweeter if I didn't say a word, so an odd anticipation grew second by second as my finger stabbed through the tracks. Then the shock as that edgy silence was broken – no instrumental intro, just straight into the lyrics:

Close my eyes and try to sleep,
Her face won't let me be.
Each night I see her in my dreams,
Each night she cuts me free.

'That's a Don Jennings song,' said Dad, genuinely surprised. 'But it's not him singing it.'

'It's legal to sing other people's songs.' The victorious can afford a touch of sarcasm.

The track continued, not the happiest of tunes, downright melancholy really, the sad lament of its lyrics soaking into the upholstery. Guy loses girl – guy is devastated, and the music caught the mood in a way that made me listen for the chords. Freddy's throaty voice was perfect for the brooding bitterness of the story the song told.

How do the love-broke carry on?
Why does love hurt most when it's gone?

He croaked the chorus out as a complaint to the whole world and a curse on himself as well. Though I ejected the disc as soon as the song was over, the mood stayed in the car. Maybe it was there already.

'How's Mum?' I asked.

'Better. Don't worry about what happened today, Josh. Your mother just wants Michael to know she loves him.'

All the same, Mum's reaction left me with jelly churning in my guts. It wasn't right that she shouted those terrible things at Dad. Forget Grandma's scrapbook; those pictures and articles only tell the football side of things. The rest has come out over the years, a word or two from Grandma, or a story overheard when Mum was talking to my aunts.

There's not much doubt about what kind of man my grandfather was. His grave is out there in Rookwood somewhere. One time I was in the water at the edge of our pool when Grandma and Aunty Denise were talking on the banana lounges.

'You should go out there and make peace with him,' said Grandma. 'Leonie's done it. Erica, too.'

'They're younger than me. They don't have the same memories,' Denise answered with a bitterness that could have coated the pool with ice.

'I'd come with you,' Grandma urged. 'It's not the sort of thing I'd ask you to do alone.'

I couldn't see their faces while this was being said but Aunty Denise's voice was enough.

'If I went out there, Mum, it would be to spit on his grave.'

'Don't speak like that, Denise. He was your father after all.'

'I don't care if he was my father. The only thing he was any good at was knocking us around when he was full. And he made a fair job of it often enough. I wish Phil had knocked his block off earlier than he did.'

Down there in the water, I shivered. Michael had told me things he had picked up long before me. When Dad was fourteen, he'd tried to stop his father from hurting Grandma and the bastard had knocked him out cold. Aunty Denise was talking about what happened a year later, another story Michael had shared with me in an excited whisper.

'Dad was into football by then and he'd learned a thing or two, eh. The old man got in a rage and came at him but this time Dad sat him on his arse and when he got up he flattened him again. Mongrel bastard got the fright of his life, didn't he. Took off like a coward and started living somewhere else.'

I just couldn't imagine fighting my own father. It's not the fists and the punches, it's how it would mess with your head.

There were others who told stories about Dad. The best, or maybe that should be the worst, is Terry Vickers. He wasn't shy about what he thought of Phil Tambling. 'As good a man as you'll ever meet and the best footballer never to play for Australia.' He always managed to fit that phrase into the conversation, making Dad cringe every time. Terry liked to talk about himself.

'I was assistant to the A Grade coach in those days. Talent scout, too, of course. It was me who saw your dad when he was captain of the Under Fifteen rep side. An absolute prodigy, if ever I saw one. I made sure St George signed him up. Got him out of school and into a job, too. I tell you, by the time he was seventeen, your father was supporting his entire family.'

All this swirled round in my head as I lay in bed on Christmas night. Niggling doubts cut across the picture of my dad that those stories had built into my own mental scrapbook, the same niggles that made me work out what I thought about God. How do you know if you're doing the right thing? How did my father know? This had turned out to be something I hadn't counted on with the whole God business. So much had suddenly made sense, and the freedom at first had been so intense, so breathtaking – like throwing open the windows and doors of a stuffy house. But that freedom had taken me further, into the open, and out here there were no walls and nothing to hold on to.

chapter eight

All through Boxing Day and the weekend that followed, Hayley watched Mum like a kid worried that her favourite toy would break. She was usually the noisy one in our house, the one who shouted, 'Mum, where're my goggles?' before she'd started looking for them herself, the one who banged into the hall table every time she ran past it, as though her personal radar was on the blink. With Hayley powered-down, our house was silent as the jungle with a predator on the prowl.

It was a relief to head into the Lost Property Office on Monday and the protection of that perspex screen. The section supervisor came to see Clive about the auction as soon as we opened up. This was Mr Bale, the man who had arranged my job in the first place. Much younger than Clive, he didn't seem to take life too seriously. He tossed the blond fringe from his eyes with a flick of his head and said, 'How's the new recruit doing? Should I put him in charge?' He wasn't really speaking to Clive because he stared straight at me with a huge grin on his dial.

'A model employee. If he stays until Easter he'll have your job, Peter,' said Clive who stood with his back to us, in the open door of the safe.

The grin turned to outright laughter. 'Well, with a dad like his, what do you expect? You've told him who your dad is, haven't you, Josh?' he asked in a low, conspiratorial whisper.

I shrugged. 'Not really.'

That was too much of an invitation. Mr Bale quickly had his arm around my shoulders calling, 'Clive, Clive, come here. He hasn't told you, has he? Josh's dad is Phil Tambling, you know, the St George legend.' (Groan! Dad hates that word.) 'Your dad gave me the *best* trade-in on my old Commodore.'

Mr Bale let me go but stood close as he switched from Clive to me and said, 'Great bloke, your dad, Josh. I was a fan of his back when I was a boy. In fact, I was at Kogarah the day he scored that famous hat-trick. You've heard about that, I suppose?'

More than that, I'd watched the whole game on video at least a dozen times – never seemed to get tired of it, though Mr Bale was starting to get tiring.

'I can still remember that second try, the way he side-stepped the last two players, one after the other. I didn't think the human body could change direction so fast.' He swivelled his hips and did a little dance to demonstrate, his hands held together in front of him, as though he was holding the ball. His mouth kept moving, blah, blah, blah.

Finally he went with Clive back to the safe and after a minute or two called goodbye as he let himself out through the security door.

'Well, well, I should have guessed from your name,' said Clive, joining me at the counter. There were no customers so I was entering details into the computer from the pile of forms beside the keyboard. 'Never much of a League fan, I'm afraid, but I do remember your father.'

'You're not the only one,' I said, rolling my eyes and nodding towards the security door.

Clive's cheeks pushed up towards his eyes in one of his closed-mouth smiles. 'Don't mind Peter.'

'Oh, I don't mind. Kind of makes me feel like a celebrity, too. When I was nine or ten, Dad would take me with him to watch my brother play. Total strangers would come up to us on the sideline and ask, "Are you Phil Tambling, from St George?" It was only embarassing when a guy called Terry Vickers came with us because he'd seen every game Dad ever played and he'd go on about what fools the selectors were for never picking Phil Tambling for the Australian team.'

'I'll bet it made you proud of your dad, though, eh?'

My turn to smile, somewhat sheepishly. 'Yeah, pretty proud. I don't think Dad liked being recognised much, but when people asked which player was his son, Dad was happy to point him out. That was when Dad looked proud because Michael was a good player, captain of the Under Fifteens one year.'

Clive took two of the forms I'd finished with and added them to a thick wad held together by a vicious bulldog clip.

'What about you, Josh. Do you play footy?'

'Me! Yeah, I still play.'

He waited for me to say more but when I didn't, went on himself. 'Same position as your father?'

'Sometimes. Actually, I'm more of a utility, I play anywhere the coach wants to fit me in.' Which is a way of saying that I spend as much time on the reserves bench as on the field. 'To tell you the truth, Clive, I'm not much chop as a footballer. I don't know why I keep playing, really.'

No, that was a lie. I know exactly why I keep playing. It's because of Dad and how disappointed he was when Michael gave it away. Halfway through Year Eleven, knocking on the door of the Firsts, he suddenly says he doesn't want to play any more. So I keep playing.

At smoko on Tuesday, Clive poured his cup of tea from the thermos and went straight back to the safe. 'Pressure's on. Have to be done by tomorrow afternoon,' he explained.

Thursday was the New Year's Day holiday but the auction wasn't until the weekend. 'What about Friday?' I asked.

'The auctioneers need a whole day to make an inventory and assign lot numbers.'

I was about to turn away when I saw him pick up an item from the shelf. The way he was quickly intrigued by it caught my eye. Though his back was to me, I could tell he was holding it in front of him and studying whatever it was carefully. It wasn't a camera. I'd seen that much. What was it, a necklace or another brooch? Whatever it was, once he'd tagged the item, he didn't put it back. He slipped it into his pocket instead.

A noticeable bulge stood out through the material of his shorts when we sat down to lunch. Later, while I was typing details into the computer from the morning deliveries, he glided by silently on his way to the compactus. I heard the gentle booms as row after row was rolled aside and, counting to ten after the last movement, I ducked my head round the corner. He was nowhere to be seen, but the compactus was open at the last bay.

When he returned a few minutes later, the bulge in his pocket was gone.

What was it? Had he put the item in that mysterious suitcase? If a customer would only turn up at the counter I would have an excuse to investigate. No such luck. Today was the quietest at the counter yet. Just as well I was patient because an hour before the day's end, an even better opportunity came my way.

'Josh, I'm popping downstairs to sort out a few things. Shouldn't be more than twenty minutes.'

As soon as he was gone, I headed for the compactus, wrenching the wheels over like a helmsman turning a fleet of battleships. There was the suitcase, not hidden in any deliberate way, but simply out of place among the collapsible prams, the bassinettes and the vague stink of baby's vomit.

With the suitcase flat on the floor, I put my fingers over the spring-loaded latches to kill the sound when they flicked up. I was half-expecting a pirate's chest of jewellery but at first glance there was no jewellery at all, just some boxes and a large book. Only when I picked up the book did I see the words in flaked gold lettering, *Holy Bible*. Next to it was a music box. The classic girlie toy, I thought at first, but it was much heavier than expected and a closer look showed it was made of some expensive wood with silver-plated hinges and handles. The second box must have belonged to an artist because it held tubes of paint and a collection of brushes bound up in a dirty cloth.

Once I had these things out on the floor beside me I saw what was going on. They were camouflage. A tea towel had been laid underneath them and when I pulled it away, there was the valuable stuff: necklaces and another brooch and a diamond ring still in its box. There were a few rings, in fact, none of them cheap junk like Melanie Stewart wanted me to give Alicia. They would all bring decent bids at the auction, but that was just it – none of this was going to the auction, was it?

Scattered among these were some pens, all expensive looking, either fountain pens with tortoiseshell casings or elegant gold and silver affairs engraved with a name. One inscription said *Writers write*. The rest of the space was taken up by bulging envelopes stacked against the hinged side of the suitcase. Were they full of jewellery, too? My hand reached forward but before I picked up the first one, the gaudy yellow and black colours of Kodak told me what they were.

What had Clive added to the collection this morning? There was no way to tell, really. My fingers were picking aimlessly among the necklaces and chains when I sensed a figure standing in the passageway beside the compactus. Oh shit.

I reeled backwards onto my heels, worried that Clive might take a swipe at me. He was moving forward towards me, but not for that. Ignoring the tea towel, he dropped the Bible, the music box and the set of paints on top of the rest and simply closed the lid. 'These items are nothing to do with you, Josh. Forget you ever saw them.'

'There's hundreds of dollars worth of stuff in there. The jewellery should be in the safe.'

'Leave it, Josh. Don't interfere,' he said firmly. It wasn't a threat or even a warning, but the command of a sixty-year-old who expected to be obeyed.

He didn't say another thing about the suitcase all afternoon. Didn't explain, didn't tell me off for hunting back there to find it. Didn't threaten me to keep my mouth shut. It was like he said – he just wanted me to forget I'd seen it.

But I couldn't forget. On my way home that afternoon, I barely saw the stations go by. Clive was hiding valuable items – hundreds, maybe thousands of dollars worth. I didn't want him to be a thief, but the evidence was clear enough.

It seemed like an odd way to steal things but as I thought about it, I started to see why. He had to be patient, had to wait and see whether the owner turned up at the counter to claim the lost property. Everything here came in from the suburban stations. There were records, and Clive couldn't be sure that the person who came looking for an item didn't already know it had been handed in. He'd be in real trouble then, if he *had* pinched it. But so much of the lost property we handled was never claimed and who would know that better than the people who worked here every day?

Clive was smart. He picked off items when it was obvious no one would come asking for them and then he could quietly play around with the records. Look at the way items were bundled together downstairs before the auction. Easy for things to go missing, get mixed up, lost all over again.

How did he sell it? When that con man tried to claim a digital camera, Clive had talked about doing a deal in a pub. That must be it. He knew because that's exactly how he did it himself.

What a grubby life he had. He probably made an extra thousand dollars every year out of this scam. But forget the money, it was the shock of finding out that got to me. I quite liked Clive. The way he treated that guy who'd lost all his connections had been something special, something that glowed. Now this. I was gutted by it, as though he had opened me up with a carving knife and emptied me out.

t was Neven's idea to head into the Domain for the New Year's Eve concert and the fireworks afterwards, though the rest of us didn't need any encouragement. The line-up of bands was better than last year's Big Day Out and I probably would have come on my own if Neven hadn't said anything.

'Bring the girls,' he suggested, which was perfect because Alicia would want me to spend New Year's Eve with her and this way I got to hear the bands as well.

Alicia's mother dropped her round at my place and we walked to the station while it was still light. The business with Clive wouldn't leave my head so I wasn't in much of a mood for talking. Alicia didn't seem to care. She can talk enough for two of us anyway and as long as I held her hand the whole way she seemed happy.

'A kiss, quick, before the train comes,' Alicia demanded. She liked spontaneous smooches, taken in a hurry so we had to break apart quickly and smile at ourselves. It was fun when I first started going out with her.

We looked for Neven and the others in the carriages as the train pulled in, but it wasn't until we stepped aboard that I saw Gemma.

'Oh, hi,' I said more brightly than I'd said anything all day. Alicia and Gemma quickly sized each other up then discovered that they had some mutual friends, some at Our Lady's, some at Fidelis. Steve's girlfriend was there as well, though Dave was girl-less and long-faced as a result.

'Good idea to bring your sister,' I commented to Steve when the movement of the train pushed us together. 'It will show her where we're going to be in a few years, eh?'

Steve shrugged and made a face. 'Don't look at me. Neven invited her.'

That set alarm bells clanging in my head. I watched them while we swayed around in the carriage. At each stop more and more bodies piled aboard, but Neven was sticking to Gemma like a limpet. Alicia and I were shoved away from them though I could still hear Gemma's laugh and catch glimpses of her giggling at the things Neven said.

Alicia stopped talking and stood watching me instead. 'What's the matter, Josh? You weren't even listening to me just then.'

'Sorry, hard day at work.'

She seemed to accept this excuse, but it was a warning all the same and I made a thing of keeping my eyes on her face all the way to Central where we changed trains for Martin Place.

Once we were in the Domain and the bands started up, no one could talk anyway. Alicia's shoulders pressed against my chest as I held her loosely around the waist. She relaxed, her hips swaying a little, moving us both as the noise burst over us. I liked that.

I'd had a couple of girlfriends before Alicia, but she was the first who liked to touch and be close that way. I pulled her a little tighter against me and she rested her head back on my shoulder, opening up her neck for a kiss above the collarbone. She was happiest with this kind of affection, like the stolen kisses as the train pulled into the station. For her, it's the currency of our relationship – she pays it out to me and she wants me to pay it back to her, like a game of cards with no losers.

If we had been alone I might have given Alicia the attention she wanted, but I was distracted by Neven and Gemma. They weren't standing intimately entwined like Alicia and me, but close enough to shout into each other's ear. I saw Gemma speak, and Neven laughed, open-mouthed. I bet he didn't even hear what she said.

'Are you ready?' a voice boomed out into the darkness.

The crowd played the game, answering the announcer lazily. He tried again, 'Are you ready?' demanding a more enthusiastic roar. 'Then welcome to the stage our second act tonight . . .' His voice died there because the band got tired of waiting and just launched into their opening number.

It was a song we did in Steve's garage. Neven and I had listened to it over and over on the Net, working out how to play it. Now, here it was, live; not just the lyrics and the frantic clash of the chords, but the energy of the band on stage.

The guy out front had the microphone stand between his legs, working his hands up and down it – shit, any more blatant and the cops would chuck him in a cell. The mosh pit was going crazy. Damn, I wished I was down there in the middle of it all. A spotlight swept back and forth across the heads, so many jammed together they became one creature, its skin rising and falling in a wave as the invisible bodies beneath raged and danced.

The singer's voice wasn't anything special, but my eyes locked onto him more tightly than any spotlight as he stroked the crowd, teased them, abused them, then raced across the stage to play air guitar in front of the speaker and mimicked the lead as he cranked up a solo break. His bare chest, the black mop of his hair, the sweat flying free as his head thrashed up and down – it was all part of the performance, part of the song itself. When the vocals cut in again and he came to the front of the stage, a spontaneous cheer blew the stars out of the sky until bam, with a final crashing chord, the song ended and the clapping and the screaming erupted across the audience.

Neven came over, dragging Gemma loosely by the hand in his wake. 'Awesome, absolutely awesome. Did you see him, Josh? The energy, the attitude. That's the way we have to do that number. You've got to do the vocals the way he did, dragging the audience in with you. You can't just stand there, growling at them like you do.'

Dave and Steve joined us, one each side of Neven as though

his criticism was coming from all three of them.

'But he's not playing a guitar like me. I can't rage around the stage. I'd trip over the leads or pull the jack out of the amplifier.'

'Yeah, yeah, maybe, but you've got to do something to connect with the audience a bit more.'

'Audience. We don't have one. We haven't done a single gig yet.'

This sounded angry. Hell, I was angry. Where did he get off criticising my vocals? Maybe that showed in my face, too, because Neven backed off a little and looked to Dave and Steve for support. They didn't say anything, but they didn't come to my rescue either, not even Dave.

'All I'm saying, Josh, is that when we do start getting gigs and you're out there in front of an audience, you have to connect with them, like that guy was doing.'

'And you don't think I'm doing that now?'

Neven's enthusiasm was waning and he started to look uncomfortable. 'Well, you're okay, Josh, but I don't know if you get the energy across, you know . . . like that guy.'

'It's just an act though. It's all put on. Do you think he really feels all that crap he was singing about?'

'So what if it is just an act? It's a bloody awesome act and we need to do the same. That's all I'm saying.'

I couldn't believe I was being dissed by my own guys. It was worse because it was Neven, too, and the way he was getting closer and closer to Gemma . . . With so much else going on in my head I didn't need this as well.

The flare-up wrecked things with Alicia, as well. When the band started up again, I couldn't go back to holding her and rocking along to the music. During the breaks after that I stayed quiet and she asked me again, 'What's the matter, Josh?' For a second there were a dozen mangled complaints on my tongue, all the things that burned like coal in a part of me I couldn't reach and not one of them would have made any sense to her.

'Come on.' I took Alicia's hand and led us off into the edges of the park until a line of massive fig trees blocked out the light from the stage.

'Do you want to talk about it?' she asked. It was much easier to speak now and she thought that was why I had brought her here.

'No, I don't even know what's bugging me.'

A sigh – the sound of defeat. Maybe she was hoping to coax me out of myself, but I wasn't in the mood for all that crap. Any words I might have said had gone now, so she pressed herself against me, offering a different sort of comfort.

I needed something and her softness against my body, face to face this time ignited those delicious sparks. I sat down on the cool, dry grass where she quickly joined me and I kissed her. She liked that and before long we were lying side by side in the lush darkness.

She was wearing a short skirt, loose and flouncy to keep her cool and show off her legs. On the grass, the skirt rode up on her thighs, but while we were just kissing it didn't matter. Then I went exploring as I'd done in the swimming pool.

'Don't, Josh, there might be people around, watching.'

What did I care if some geek was watching in the bushes?

'Stop it,' she said a few seconds later, but I didn't want to stop, I wouldn't stop.

She broke away from me and gave out a pathetic sob. 'Why do you always spoil it, Josh? Every time I see you now you're all over me. Why can't we just kiss a bit and talk and stuff?'

Because you don't want to talk about the stuff that interests me. But that answer never made it out into the darkness.

'Are you mad at me?' she asked when I made no reply.

'No, of course not. It's just that you get me so fired up when we're together like this.' She was still close to me, lying on her side. I reached out, resting my hand high on her hip, slipping down into the curve at the base of her rib cage. She pressed her own hand gently on top of my fingers. Safe territory.

It wasn't enough. I wanted more than safe and with barely a thought, my hand slipped up onto her breast, the softness of her lighting up my blood.

Alicia rolled away instantly and stood up, brushing the grass from her skirt and legs. It was all I could do to stifle the groan that rumbled deep in my guts. I might have said something stupid then, something to hurt her and end our relationship in a single savage cut. But I didn't.

'I'm sorry,' were the words that came automatically. 'I thought that . . .'

What did I think? This night was going from bad to worse and there didn't seem to be anything I could do about it.

And Alicia was on the verge of giving me both barrels.

'Even when you have your arm around me you're looking somewhere else,' she said bitterly. 'It could be anyone here on the ground with you, couldn't it? Wouldn't matter to you!'

'No, that's not it at all,' I blurted out, appalled that she was so close to the truth. 'Even if I can't see your face in the darkness, I know it's you and that's all that matters to me. And what happened just now, it's to show how much you mean to me. It wouldn't do anything for me if it wasn't you.'

Where did those words come from?

Her silence told me she was thinking about this. 'Well, there are better ways of showing how much you like me,' she sniffed, smoothing her clothes all over again, for show this time. I was still surprised by my own words and wondered whether I was overdoing it, saying so much more than I felt. Then a spotlight from the stage hundreds of metres away swept the trees and for an instant Alicia's legs and the perfect curve of her hips were caught in silhouette. The urge to touch her, to draw her down beside me again was almost too much to resist.

'Alicia,' I said tentatively. 'I'm sorry, it hasn't been much of a night for you. I do care so much about you and that's why I get so excited when we're alone like this. You're the best thing that's ever happened to me. It's true! And I don't want to lose you because of tonight, I don't want to lose you ever,' I pleaded and taking a risk, I reached up and took hold of her hand.

She didn't snatch it away, and when I tugged gently, she bent towards me, folding herself low enough for our lips to meet in a kiss. Her hand stayed in mine until she was beside me once more on the grass. I folded my arms around her in a show of affection, careful where our bodies touched, conscious of how my hands pressed her against me and nothing more. The stiffness left her muscles and after lingering in this specially crafted embrace for a few moments, she lifted her face from my chest and said, 'Do I really mean that much to you?'

'More than the band, more than music itself,' I whispered, amazed that the words were so easy to say. She monitored my movements minutely as I pressed my lips to her ear and said, 'I love you so much,' and then I kissed her tenderly below the ear lobe. Her arms slipped around my back and she hugged me with the same tenderness.

'I like it when we kiss, Josh, and I like the other things, too, really I do, but . . . you come on too strong and don't give me a chance to . . . to work out what I feel. And out here in the park, it's so public . . . not like I want it to be.'

'How do you want it to be?' I asked, content to follow the conversation wherever she wanted it to go, as long as she stayed beside me. While she considered her answer, my lips brushed her neck and then the base of her throat.

'Somewhere warm and cosy. That's how I want it to be,' she murmured. 'Just you and me and nothing to worry about.'

With my hands behaving themselves, Alicia let herself enjoy the intimacy of my caresses. She began to run her own hands slowly up and down my back, holding me as much as I was holding her. My lips had worked lower, to the neckline of her top, but I didn't push my luck.

'We could find somewhere,' I said.

'Yeah, we could,' she responded lazily and we went back to kissing.

Almost a minute passed, then Alicia turned her mouth away and whispered, 'I'm not getting pregnant, though, no way. You have to take care of that, okay?'

What was she talking about? At first I wanted to stop the tape and run back through our conversation to pick out what I had missed. But as I forced back the initial shock, her meaning was plain enough and to ask her to spell it out would spoil the moment. She might even change her mind altogether.

'Where *can* we go, though,' I asked, cringing at the urgency in my voice, but the fever opening up in my head no longer cared what I sounded like. 'We can't exactly sneak into my bedroom at this time of night, or yours for that matter and . . .'

'Not tonight, Josh,' she said with a nervous laugh. 'I'm just saying, you know, I love you, too, and the whole boyfriend, girlfriend thing. If anything's going to happen, it has to be . . . well, I've said, haven't I.'

We broke apart soon after and stood up, helping each other straighten our clothes and brush away the creases. Back among the noise and energy of the concert, the others hardly knew we'd been gone, except Dave who gave me a brief look, half lewd suggestion, half envy. Thank God he didn't know what had just happened between Alicia and me. I could hardly believe it myself.

She was happy, now that I was affectionate and attentive, touching her the way she liked to be touched, making her laugh and whispering things in her ear, words I thought up just to make her happy. They were like the lyrics of a song, not really mine and so I wasn't responsible for their meaning. As the singer had done on stage, I used them for the effect they created.

It didn't bug me so much then that Neven was snuggling closer and closer to Gemma. At midnight, they kissed openly, a long, lingering New Year's pash – but what did I care? I had Alicia and the promise of the weeks ahead, if I could find some place to take her.

chapter ten

I fell asleep thinking of Alicia and the next morning my eyes hadn't been open for ten seconds before I was think-ing of her again. Well, not her so much, but what she'd said, what she'd hinted at, what she'd left me thinking about. Couldn't get it out of my head. This was the first day of a new year, the time for starting over but my mind was held back by Alicia and even if I'd been able to push her aside there was still Clive and the stuff in that suitcase. I wandered aimlessly around the house until Mum chewed me out.

'What's the matter with you? You're like a bear with a sore head.'

'I'm tired from last night.'

'Then for God's sake, go back to bed,' she growled.

Dad looked up from his plate. If he started asking questions I might say something about Clive and then have to explain. It wouldn't be the first time that I'd blurted out what was worry-ing me to Dad. It usually happened when he was driving me somewhere in the car. Sometimes he didn't even say a word, or offer any advice, not even a murmur of sympathy, but whatever was bugging me would become easier to handle because I'd told him. But we hadn't talked like that for a while. There was something in the way.

I went back to bed, like Mum suggested, and lay awake tossing back and forth until the solution finally came to me: I had to find a way to stop Clive's grubby scam. Only then did I sleep.

The train was late getting into Central on Friday morning. Clive said nothing – about me being late or what had happened before the New Year's break. The auctioneers had arrived downstairs and he spent the morning with them, leaving me to handle the counter alone. He came back for lunch bringing with him a guy about Dad's age who sported a huge gut straining the buttons of his crumpled business shirt. How could he wear a tie in weather like this?

'This is Josh, my offsider while Maurie's on his honeymoon,' Clive said to the man. 'Josh, this is Mr Witworth who'll be calling the auction tomorrow.'

While he was introducing us a customer had come down the ramp, so I stayed at the counter, but I could hear them talking.

'I see you still bring the thermos, Clive.'

'Yes, would you like a cup?'

'Wouldn't say no,' said Mr Witworth with a laugh in his voice that meant he had been fishing for the offer. Damn, these two were mates. They'd probably been doing these auctions together for years. That was going to ruin what I had in mind. I went out to the kiosk for my own lunch and by the time I returned they had started listing all the valuables from the safe on Mr Witworth's clipboard.

My plan seemed to have been thwarted until a new face arrived, Dad's grateful client, Mr Bale. He called a brisk 'G'day,' in my direction then let himself in through the security door. The easy joking between Clive and Mr Witworth stopped as soon as he joined them at the safe.

Here was my chance. I slipped away unnoticed and took Clive's secret stash out from behind the prams. After releasing the catches, I stood up and lifted the open suitcase into my arms with the lid falling back against my chest.

'Clive, look at this lot,' I called, loading my voice with urgency and surprise. All three gaped at me as I emerged from the compactus. 'I found it just now in with the prams and baby gear. Is there any stuff here that should go into the auction?'

'No,' said Clive. This sounded like an answer to my question but I think it was more the shock of seeing me with his precious suitcase. 'There's nothing for this auction left in the compactus,' he said, recovering quickly and he started towards me, intent on forcing me back out of the way.

'This stuff looks pretty old though, Clive. You might have missed it. Shouldn't you look, just in case?' I suggested, keeping up the act.

Mr Witworth was convinced. Without a glance at Clive he called, 'Bring it here, let me see.'

As soon as he spotted the few pieces of jewellery I'd spread out on top of the Bible, he was hooked. He took a silver locket on a chain and read the tag. 'February! This one should have been auctioned in July, Clive.'

Clive spun round to face him. His friend was betraying him without realising and now his eyes shot to Mr Bale who was watching all this without saying a word. If Clive resisted any more he risked giving himself away. 'Yes, should have,' he muttered. 'That case must have been shoved in the wrong bay and forgotten about.' He was careful to sound as though someone else had made the mistake. Mr Bale swallowed the offhand explanation without a whimper.

'You've got enough for tomorrow's auction, Errol,' Clive said to Mr Witworth. 'No need to rush things. There's paperwork to do with this lot. All takes time. Why not leave it until midyear?'

The auctioneer stopped poking his podgy fingers through the treasure trove. He'd picked up the reluctance in his mate's voice now. 'Another dozen lots is not going to make much difference, but if you want to hold these over, Clive, it's up to you.'

But it wasn't up to Clive after all: Mr Bale was the supervisor and it was his call. 'Put them in this auction, Errol,' he instructed. 'There's time to do the paperwork this afternoon.'

What could Clive say? His bluff had just been called. I had won. There wasn't even going to be any awkward moments or accusations of stealing. I hadn't wanted that to happen. I just wanted to beat Clive, to cheat the cheat – and I had done it.

I looked Clive full in the face. He was angry, of course he was, but there wasn't the fury I'd expected, of a thief who had seen his prizes snatched away from under his nose. He broke the stare first, dropping his eyes to the items that Mr Witworth had taken from the suitcase and laid out on the table for closer inspection. Yes, there was an undeniable loss in his stance, the folded arms, the tight jaw. Gotcha.

But the smirk that came with this triumph died on my face when those eyes turned to me a second time. I had thwarted a thief so why did his eyes spear right through my chest? His expression was impossible to read.

'We'll give Lot Numbers to the jewellery and a few other things,' said Mr Witworth. 'But the rest of it's worthless. What do you want to do with the junk, Clive? And those photographs. No point taking personal snapshots down to the auction.'

'I'll toss 'em in the garbage, then,' he answered, his eyes breaking away from me at last. The suitcase wasn't wanted either, so he closed it silently with the bundles of photographs inside, but since it was too large for our rubbish bin, he simply placed it out of the way, against the wall.

chapter eleven

Saturday is *the* day at Dad's showroom and, as he always does, he left about seven to go over the newspapers at his desk before the phone started to ring. The deep purr of his Statesman's engine woke me. The auction didn't start until nine so I could punch out Zs for another hour; I rolled over. Next thing I knew, my watch was telling me it was ten o'clock.

Charging into the kitchen with a shirt still over my head, I found Mum at the table, a cup of coffee in front of her and the car keys near her left hand. 'Are you taking Hayley somewhere? I should have been in town an hour ago.'

'I took her to squad training. Have to pick her up again at eleven-thirty if that's any use.' She took a sip from her cup. 'Do you want a coffee, Josh?'

'No, no, just this,' I said, shaking the packet of Nutri-Grain I'd grabbed from the cupboard.

She had been halfway out of her chair but she shrugged

and settled again. There was no newspaper spread out in front of her, just the coffee. She watched me, obviously about to say something. Her hesitation dusted an odd tension over my cereal until she came up with the words.

'Hayley said you two had a talk about Michael on Christmas Day. I'm glad you talked about him. She's too young to remember, but there were happier times with Michael. I have to keep telling myself that.' She paused and took a sip of her coffee to steady herself. 'Look, what happened after he called, that was my fault . . .'

I glanced at my watch. It was really not a good time for this, but I let the spoonful of cereal splash back into the bowl. 'It's okay. I understand why those calls stir you up.'

'Yes, but I want to say I'm sorry anyway, Josh. I've hardly spoken to you since Christmas, except to snap at you on New Year's Day. I'm sorry about that, sorry about everything.'

If she went on like this she would apologise for the famine in Africa. 'It's all right, Mum. Look, I didn't get a chance to tell you the other day. Michael sounded pretty happy when he rang. He was having a great time, wherever he was.'

Hurt and confused, she stared back at me, as though my words had been stones tossed carelessly against her forehead. I'd said the wrong thing again, hadn't I? Damn. If Michael really was happy, he wouldn't want to be here right now. The smile would slide right off his face.

With both elbows propped on the table and looking down between them, Mum began to rub her forehead. Then she seemed to worry how this might look to me and pretended to scratch an imaginary itch above her nose.

'It's a shame he wasn't here for his twenty-first, you know. It's not something you put off to another time.'

'You can still give him a present when he comes home.'

'Yes, that's true. Yes, a present,' she repeated, not quite convinced. 'This bangle was Joanne's twenty-first birthday present from our parents.' With a little tugging and squeezing, she worked the heavy golden band free over her knuckles. 'See the inscription.' She pointed it out as she passed the bangle across the table. 'Joanne loved that bangle. Wore it every day.'

Silence again. Shovelling Nutri-Grain in fast forward, I checked the time on the clock behind Mum's head. If I caught the 10:26 from Oatley I would still see part of the auction and since the items in Clive's suitcase were added at the last minute, they might be the last things sold as well.

'Joanne was with me the first time I saw Dad play footy. Did you know that, Josh?'

Of course I knew. It was part of our family folklore, the day Phil Tambling scored three tries in the one game against South Sydney, the only hat-trick of his career and just by coincidence, Mum was a spectator in the crowd. Three years would pass before they met in that fateful radio interview and started going out together.

Mum drained her cup and played with it between her hands, barely noticing what she was doing. *Please, Mum, no more of the old stories I'd heard a hundred times. Not now, I've got to get going.*

'That day has always meant more to me than Dad's three tries, though.'

This was new. Mum had never gone beyond the famous facts before. I had finished my cereal but between her voice and the weight of her eyes, transferred from the empty coffee cup to my face now, I felt tied to my chair. 'She'd always been just my younger sister until then, too young to talk to about some things, but the day your father was the hero of Kogarah it was different. We started to become more like best friends. I've been thinking about it lately, the irony. Twenty-five years later and the sister beside me in the stand that day is dead. Instead, the closest person in my life is a man who was out there on the field. Didn't even know his name until he scored those three tries.'

Her eyes went back to the cup in her hands. 'Father McHugh says it can take two years to get over the death of someone close to you.' Then after a pause she said, 'Michael's been gone more than two years.'

'He's not dead, Mum.'

'No, no, of course not,' she agreed quickly.

More silence. The memories seemed spent. I moved cautiously to the dishwasher, my mind already jumping ahead, calculating how fast I would have to run to make that train. Then Mum spoke again. 'Do you want a cup of coffee, Josh?'

What was this obsession with coffee? She'd already asked me once. I started to refuse until the sight of her body huddled listlessly at the kitchen table choked off the words in my throat. The house would be empty once I left, empty except for Mum and she wasn't quite here this morning, not all of her. Hadn't been for months.

'Yeah, Mum, I'll have a coffee. Do you want another one yourself?'

'I'll make them,' she insisted, coming to life.

I sat down again and let her get on with it.

Mum dropped me at Oatley on her way to collect Hayley from swimming training. Even with me urging the sluggish carriages out of every station, we didn't pull into Central until midday. From the platform it was a sprint through the tunnels and out onto Eddy Street, past the bus terminal to arrive panting in Pitt Street.

People lingered outside the green door but I quickly sensed the air of a party that was already over. A woman emerged into the sunlight carrying the bargains she had picked up, an old radio-cassette player in one hand, a lime-green shopping bag of clothes in the other.

I slipped through the heavy door anyway and immediately fell under the suspicious eye of a beefy security guard. Let him look – I wasn't the thief here. Sounds echoed around the cavernous room in a different way from my earlier visit and the reason was obvious enough. The shelves and the benches, so crowded with junk only yesterday, were now laid bare with just the odd lonely item remaining, first lost on a train and now rejected by the bidders. Next stop for them was the dumpster outside.

Amid the echoes it was easy to spot Mr Witworth who

stood with a female assistant, both of them focused intently on a clipboard. I waited until the young woman moved away then took her place at his side. My luck was holding up because he recognised my face.

'How did it go?' I asked.

'Fair result, can't complain,' he sighed, hitching up his pants beneath that enormous paunch and flicking the clipboard with his forefinger. 'If you're looking for Clive, he's gone upstairs.'

'I'll see him Monday, I suppose. Actually, I was interested in how those last few things sold. You know, the stuff from that suitcase.'

'Here, see for yourself,' he offered, handing me the clipboard. The assistant was back with two glasses of water, passing one to Mr Witworth and gulping the other herself. No wonder, because it was stifling in here.

I worked quickly before Mr Witworth took back the clipboard. It held page after page of lists. Starting with the lot number on the left-hand side, there was a wide column under the heading Item Description, then two much narrower columns marked Bidder's No. and Sale Price.

The first page started with cameras then switched to jewellery which extended onto the second page. I looked for the jewellery that had come from the suitcase but there was no way to tell one brooch or necklace or ring from the rest. Some had gone for hundreds of dollars.

After the jewellery came the electrical goods, then music – everything from a guitar and the flute I'd seen to the CDs. Clothing filled up the rest until the last page finished off with the real junk, the odds and ends. This time I did recognise items from the suitcase, the very last ones sold:

Lot 369 – Five pens, 2 b/point, 3 fountain		
(various brands)	79	$15
Lot 370 – Leather-bound Bible	79	$5
Lot 371 – Tubes of oil paint in box	79	$12
Lot 372 – Music Box. Antique Austrian	79	$65

The final column showed the price and a quick calculation in my head said they had brought less than a hundred dollars in total. Without the jewellery to add in this seemed a pathetic amount of money. Why would Clive want to steal these things, anyway, when apart from the music box they were practically worthless?

Coming here today was supposed to be a victory. I'd wanted to see all the things Clive was holding back for himself go under the hammer and the money end up in the proper hands. When I finally looked at what he was hoarding, reduced to words on a page, my stomach twisted. There was something going on here that I hadn't seen.

This uneasiness made me study the list more closely and that was when I saw it, number 79, entered in one of the columns for all of the items from the suitcase.

'Mr Witworth,' I asked. He had sent the young woman for another glass of water, but turned his head now to hear my question. 'This column, bidder's number. What does it mean?'

He swivelled right round to face me. 'Tells us who bought each item. We use numbers instead of names to speed things up. See that card?' He pointed three metres away to a bright orange square of thin cardboard that had been trampled into the floor. It was about twenty centimetres along each side but despite the grubby shoe prints I could make out a large black number in the centre, 133. 'All bidders have to register and we give them a card like that with a number.'

'So if these four things on the end of the list have the same number, then they were all bought by the same person.'

He took the clipboard from my hand and glanced at where I was holding back the top pages to keep the last page exposed. 'Yep, dead right. In fact, I can even tell you who number seventy-nine was. You know him, of course . . .'

I'd guessed before he said the name.

'. . . Clive Staples.'

chapter **twelve**

'**L**ouder, Josh. Get angry.'

Yeah, well, that wasn't going to be hard if Neven kept this up. We were rehearsing again at Steve's place on Saturday afternoon, though thankfully the summer heat was taking a rest for the day. That didn't mean I wasn't in a lather of sweat as we tried to get through another song by Bluntblade without stuffing up the timing or the music itself. I could kill Dave. About time he learned to handle that bass like a professional.

The frustration was enough without Neven going on like a demented record producer. Some of it was an act he was putting on for Gemma's benefit, because she was there, looking gorgeous, even with her hair tied back untidily in a single elastic band and wearing a loose T-shirt over a pair of footy shorts. (Shorts never looked *that* good on a footballer.)

But I had to keep my mind on the vocals. 'Here, give me the guitar,' Neven insisted and before I could protest he had lifted the Fender's strap over my head. 'Just do the singing.'

'It'll sound pretty thin without any rhythm guitar holding the thing together.'

'Have a go anyway, Josh.'

He nodded at Steve who led us into this number with his drums, then Dave and Neven started up together until the intro was over and I had to come in hard with the words.

I sang. No, I yelled. Neven was standing in front of me, working his guitar, encouraging me, or maybe cajoling is a better word. The overall sound was definitely missing the strong chords of my Fender, but I put this out of my mind and belted out the words. The frustration of the past few days fed into my voice until it became harsher, even angry, just as Neven wanted. I grabbed the microphone, like the singer on New Year's Eve, and bellowed the chorus.

I see right through you baby,
Your lies don't work on me.
You didn't want the love I gave,
Today I'm breaking free.

Neven gave a little whoop, as though he was saying, 'Go for it, Josh.'

So I kept it up, wrenching words up from my lungs with an energy that was foreign to me, screeching about the world and what it had done to me: shutting me out, denying me a place, forcing me to the edge. The strange thing was that it wasn't so hard. All I had to do was put on an act, as though the words actually meant something to me and soon the attitude they generated seemed to take on a physical presence through me that I projected out to the audience. The audience was just the guys in my own band and Gemma who stood still with her back resting against the bare brick wall. I tried even harder. It was a wonder my eyeballs didn't pop right out of their sockets.

It was working, though, and Neven let me go at it while he turned his attention to his guitar work, mixing his lead with the chords usually supplied by my Fender. Gemma pushed off the wall and began to dance in front of him. She came closer than last time, turning in slow circles and letting the neck of his guitar brush her shoulder and even trace a line down her back when she faced away from him.

She liked that, shimmying her narrow hips as though the touch of the polished wood had sent shivers up her spine. She worked herself round to smile at him, open-eyed and open-mouthed but just when it seemed she was going to jump all over him, guitar and all, she turned to me, dancing just as provocatively and with her face still wide with the wild freedom of the moment. Watching her so close, the deepest longing cut through me – for love, for sex, for the kind of bliss that has a hundred names and none good enough to describe it.

The song's lyrics died away, leaving Neven the centre of attention again as he thrashed out the heavy chords that ended the song. Desperate to stay part of the action, I hammed it up with him, raising my arms triumphantly above my head for a second then bending forward and swinging my hair close to his reverberating guitar, showering him and Gemma with sweat.

'That's the way. You did it, Josh,' Neven cried.

Dave broke into enthusiastic whooping and Steve dropped his drumsticks to clap with both hands above his head, Gemma, too, but in a half-hearted way, as though I'd earned a highly commended at some primary school eisteddfod.

'Do you all want a Coke to celebrate?' she asked.

Since I was the only one free of an instrument, I went with her into the house to fetch the drinks. She handed three cans up to me from a shelf low down in the fridge but the fourth one she popped and held out towards me then opened another for herself. We weren't going straight back to the garage, it seemed.

'You don't like it, do you, Josh?' she said once she'd swallowed. 'That kind of singing, I mean. You don't like doing it that way.'

'I did okay. The other guys seemed to think so.'

'Yeah, you were good, really good by the end. I'll bet you can do just about anything when you put your mind to it, specially if someone like Neven pushes you hard enough. But it's not you, you're not that kind of singer.'

'With these songs you have to be. Goes with the territory.'

She shrugged, as though my answer had disappointed her and immediately I wanted another chance. I didn't want this girl disappointed with me; I wanted to impress her, wanted her to like me, talk to me, flash that confident open-mouthed smile of hers and send sparks skittering across my skin.

She felt for the bench behind her and sprang backwards

onto it, an easy movement she'd done a thousand times. 'I've been thinking about what you told me the other night, about God, about not believing.'

This was a quick change of subject, though maybe it wasn't so far from what we'd been talking about. 'You're the only person I've ever told.'

Her face brightened. 'It's not something anyone talks about much, is it? You just take it for granted that most people believe in some kind of God.'

'I told you why I don't.'

'I know, and that's what I've been working over in my head. You see, I don't agree with you about the rest of the Universe being a waste. God can still take an interest in us, here on Earth.'

'There's more to it than that.'

'Yeah, well, I guessed there would be. But I like the idea of a God watching over us. It's a comfort, especially when something bad happens.' Then she laughed at herself, or at both of us, really, aware of what we were talking about and the earnest tone in our voices. 'I don't think about it much, really. Nobody does.'

'I do.'

She backtracked immediately, reached forward until she was almost overbalanced in order to touch my arm. I jumped at the coldness of her fingertips. 'I didn't mean to sound like that, Josh. Maybe people do think about it but nobody *talks* about it much. School is about the only place and even then we just jump through the hoops the teachers hold up for us.'

She was right about that. Until I started watching the night sky and reading and wondering, those hoops were all I ever jumped through. Too easy. 'Does it make any difference to what you do though, Gemma?'

'What I do! In my ordinary life, you mean?' She pondered the question with the same seriousness that I liked so much about her. 'Hard to tell. The things I do each day are just the way I am.'

Dave burst in from the garage. 'What happened to the Cokes you promised? Come on, Josh. Neven wants to do another song to see if you can sing the same way again.'

Back with the guys, I tried with my guitar strapped on, though with the aggression I was pouring into the lyrics, my hands pounded too hard on the strings, loosing the clarity of the chords. Neven stayed off my back, at least, and he seemed much happier, thrashing his guitar with the same energy I was cranking out into the microphone.

But Gemma was right. I didn't like what was happening. The only way I could get through the session was to separate out the performance from myself until I became a spectator, watching myself go at it. That wasn't really me pouring out all that bitterness and fury at the world. Yes, it was my voice, but not my words, or anything like what I was feeling.

Gemma watched me put on the act. She knew. She even winked at me when I really went to town on the last song. But afterwards, it was Neven she took a fresh can of Coke to and it was his lame jokes she laughed at. There was no doubt she liked him, liked being around him, flirting with him in that way that girls have when they know they've got a guy interested. But there was something about the way we had connected before in the kitchen. Okay, it was serious stuff and nobody wants to sound so solemn all the time, but she cared about what we were saying and she cared even more that I'd trusted her to hear it.

'Six days to go,' said Dave from behind me as I stood watching Neven and Gemma. I was still thinking about our conversation and took a moment to catch on.

'Port Macquarie, you idiot,' he blurted into my bewildered face as I turned to face him.

'Sure, can't wait,' I said automatically.

'Listen, I thought we should have a little farewell party on Friday night. Get a few girls around, eh? We could do it at my place.'

'Your place!' Dave's house wasn't exactly the social hot spot of planet Earth.

'Yeah, Mum and Dad are going to Bega for the weekend to stay with some friends. What they don't know won't hurt them.'

To be honest I wasn't that enthusiastic and tried to let him down gently. 'I don't know how many girls we'll get, a lot of them are away on holiday.'

'You could ask Alicia to bring her mates, though, eh? We'll have the place to ourselves, remember.' He dug me in the ribs and contorted his face into a leer. 'No parents and lots of empty bedrooms.'

*

Sunday had hurried round again. My mind always wandered during Mass, even when I went along with the whole thing. But once I started to suspect the big con, this quiet, intensely personal hour among the pews became a chance to do the heavy lifting inside my head. I even looked forward to it in a strange way, because nobody knew what I was thinking. Once I'd made up my mind and didn't need to work things out any longer, Mass became a hole in time, like I'd pressed the pause button on my life from eight o'clock until nine every Sunday.

That Sunday was different. I couldn't stop thinking about Clive. Why had he bought back those pieces of junk at the auction? And when Mr Witworth had let me make another brief check of the lists yesterday, I'd found number 79 in the Bidder's column for some of the jewellery too. What kind of crook pays for the things he wants to steal? I couldn't work it out, and while I pondered over that, my mind kept hurling other thoughts at me from so many different directions until standing in silence became almost unbearable.

It occurred to me that my silence and my place next to Dad was just another act. This was my Sunday performance, like the show I had put on in the garage yesterday afternoon, roaring out the songs that Neven had chosen.

Actor, I seethed at myself. Worse than an actor – you're a fraud.

It wasn't supposed to be like this. I'd stood in this church for months now, knowing there was no God up there listening to the prayers and the cheesy hymns. There's something triumphant in being so sure of what you believe, or in my case, what

I don't believe. It's settled into my bones now, become part of me. I couldn't go back now, wasn't even tempted, but all the same, I hadn't counted on mornings like this when an emptiness opened up inside me despite my rock-solid certainty. Though I was sure God was never there, when I finally let go of all the crap, something else disappeared, too.

I looked at people around me, all devoted to an elaborate myth. I pitied them for their delusions but in a ridiculous way I envied them, too. They weren't the ones calling themselves a fraud. They could make a kind of peace for themselves out of something, even though it didn't exist. I won't do that, I can't, but I want that peace all the same.

chapter thirteen

I was waiting at the door when Clive came down the ramp on Monday morning. We didn't speak. It was as if I wasn't there at all. And part of me wished I wasn't. After punching in the security code, Clive made straight for the round table where he sat the thermos in its customary position and put his plastic lunch box in the fridge.

Only when the familiar ritual was complete did I see the suitcase pushed under the table. Clive saw me staring at it and the silence between us intensified until I couldn't bear it any longer.

'I spoke to Mr Witworth after the auction. Bidder seventy-nine, it was you. You bought back everything from the suitcase,' I said, bewildered and miserable. My eyes stayed focused on the suitcase because I couldn't look him in the face.

'Not everything,' Clive replied, wary of words, like I had been. 'Some of the jewellery was too expensive. I managed to get a couple of necklaces and a brooch like the one that lady came looking for in your first week.'

At last I dared look at him and this seemed to make it easier for him. His shoulders loosened and, leaning on the seat of a chair, he pulled out the suitcase, placing it gently on the table. The catches made a flick-thud sound, one after the other as he released them and raised the lid. There were the music box and the Bible on top, and the ancient tea towel hiding the smaller items below.

'Why didn't you take all these things home on Saturday? There're yours now. You paid for them.'

'No, all these things belong to someone else. That's what the Lost Property Office is for, to get lost things back to their owners.'

'But how can people claim stuff when you're hiding it?'

Clive sighed. 'I was only hiding it so that it wouldn't be auctioned off for a few dollars. I can't let them go, not yet.' He hesitated, searching for words again. His head and neck receded even further into his shoulders and when he finally spoke, it was as though he was pleading with me to understand.

'I've been working here more than twenty years, Josh. You get to know after a while, you get a feeling about the things people will come looking for.'

'But if you lose something, you go looking for it straight away, don't you? If you don't, it's gone forever.'

'Not always. It's not that way for everyone.'

He seemed suddenly self-conscious at the way we still

stood, facing each other. 'Sit down, Josh,' he said and posi-
tioned a chair at the table for me. He sat on the other chair and
pulled the thermos towards him.

'Do you want a cup?'

I remembered Mum on Saturday morning with the coffee.
It was a comfort thing, a prop to ease conversation. I nodded.

Clive fetched a second cup from the sink and once he'd
poured us each a tea, he started up again.

'Not everyone leads a simple life like you and me, Josh.
Things go wrong for them. Some of the items that end up
here weren't left behind out of forgetfulness or confusion.
Sometimes a person is taken off a train, by the police or rail
security. They end up in gaol or a psychiatric ward. They
might not sound like the best people, Josh, but some of them
need what they've lost more than the ones who come in here
for their umbrellas or a mobile phone.'

'The creepy guy, just before Christmas,' I said immediately. 'He was looking for his diary, with addresses and phone
numbers.'

Clive nodded. 'Yes, he'd lost part of himself somehow and
that diary would have helped him get it back. But his bag was
never handed in. I was certain of that as soon as he described
it.'

'You remember!'

'Things like that, I remember. It's like I said, you get a feel
for things.'

I looked down at the music box and the rest. The empty
space around them accused me. Oh God, what had I done?

'The jewellery you couldn't afford, it's gone now, lost, thanks to me.' The guilt was crushing me. 'How much did you spend? I'll pay you back the money.'

'No, Josh, don't be ridiculous.'

'But I messed it all up for you. You're trying to help people and I got in the way.'

'It's not your fault, Josh. I shouldn't have let you see the suitcase.'

I pressed him harder about the money until he snapped, 'Stop it, Josh. Keep your money for the music you play with your friends.'

An awkward silence followed but I was full of questions. 'How do you know what to keep and what to let go?'

Clive sat back with the mug of tea, eyebrows pulled tightly downwards as he took his time to answer. 'It's not easy to explain. When an item is handed in, I might hear about its circumstances and occasionally things will come in after an incident, you know, an arrest that gets reported in the papers. But mostly it's intuition. Here, I'll show you something,' he said eagerly.

Bending forward again and setting his tea carefully on the table, he took out the Bible then, from beneath it, the box of paints. Releasing the tiny snib, he opened it to reveal the tubes of oil colour and a collection of brushes wrapped in a strip of dirty cloth. But this wasn't what he was showing me. 'See the inside of the lid.'

He turned it towards me, careful to keep the lid upright so I could see the inside.

'A portrait!'

'Yes, painted directly onto the wood, but look at it, Josh.'

Oh, I was looking all right. The woman in the portrait was naked, or topless at least because she had been painted from the waist up. Her body was turned away slightly, leaving her small breasts in profile, but her face was painted full on to the viewer, a proud face captured in a moment of ease and contentment.

'He loved her,' I said spontaneously.

'Ah,' Clive sighed. 'You see it, too. Do you understand now why I couldn't let it go so quickly? If you had painted this, wouldn't you grieve for its loss? Wouldn't you want it back, even if you had left it behind deliberately, even if it brought you pain?'

My eye fell on the photographs. They were all in pristine condition, except for the slight discolouration of age on one or two. 'You had all of these developed yourself, didn't you?'

'Yes,' Clive confirmed. 'I do it because of what happened once. There was a train crash, four years ago, a dozen people dead. All of the unclaimed items ended up here, one of them a camera, a Nikon SLR. No one claimed it and it was sold at the next auction. Then nearly a year later, a woman turned up at the counter. Because the camera came from the accident, I remembered and I had to tell her it was gone. But she didn't care about the camera, Josh, she wanted the film inside it. Her son and her grand-daughter had been on a day out together at Taronga Park. Those pictures would have been precious to that family. Ever since then, if there's a lot of shots used up in a camera, I have the film developed and keep the photos in there.'

'Have you ever returned any of the pictures?'

'Once. It happened once,' he answered immediately, and from the joy in his face, it must have been quite a buzz.

'You think I'm a crazy old man, don't you, Josh?'

'No, not at all, not at all,' I repeated. I really wanted him to believe me.

'I do it for myself, Josh, as much as anyone else,' he confessed, glancing down at the photos. 'Oh, I don't kid myself that it's very important, but I've got no one close to me any more, to do anything special for. No wife, kids gone and taking care of themselves, my grandchildren out of reach. I don't feel like I'm alive unless I'm doing some good in the world.'

The thumping echoes of footsteps on the ramp told us we had a customer.

'Put the suitcase away for me, would you, Josh?' Clive asked as he headed for the counter.

chapter fourteen

'What was the first thing you put away in the suitcase?' I asked Clive at smoko.

'A letter, actually. A love letter.'

'Romantic?'

'I don't know. Couldn't read it,' he said with a smile that would have done Dave Zilly proud. 'It was written in Italian, you see, but my neighbour in Strathfield was born in Naples and he said it was moving and heartfelt, that it came from a woman who couldn't migrate here until her grandmother died.'

Clive took a bite from his sandwich and chewed slowly. Did he know that I was hooked? Was he drawing out the story to tease me, some kind of old-guy payback for what I had done?

'I could just see a lonely man sitting on the train, reading the letter then putting it down on the seat beside him.'

'Did he come for it?'

'Oh yes. He walked past our sign every day on his way to

work. But the words are in English. It was three months before it dawned on him what they might mean.'

'And you had his letter waiting in your suitcase.'

'In a drawer. Only started with the suitcase when I needed to keep pieces of jewellery out of the auction.'

'Was that letter the best thing you've ever returned?'

'They don't all tell me their stories, Josh. Besides, who can guess what a person is feeling on the other side of that perspex? That's not why I do it.'

'But you said you do it for yourself. Whatever they feel, you share in it.'

'Do I? No, if I feel good, well, that comes from this side of the screen, from me. Warms my tired old soul, you might say.' He laughed at himself as he munched more of the sandwich.

'You don't strike me as the religious type, Clive.'

He frowned and thought back over what he had said while he swallowed. 'Oh, the soul. Just an expression, Josh. No, I'm not one for any of that stuff.'

'Neither am I,' I assured him quickly.

'It's amazing what people put a value on, though. I didn't realise until I started making my own educated guesses. You've seen the items in that suitcase. Nothing terribly valuable. That brooch the woman came for in your first week was the same. Even *she* knew it wouldn't interest a jeweller. It's the sentimental value, the emotions they connect to, the memories. It can feel like you're giving people back a part of their lives.'

A delicious ache began then in my chest and, leaning

forward, I said, 'If anyone comes in, anyone looking for your special stuff, you'll tell me, won't you?'

His face creased solemnly and though he didn't actually sigh, he had that air about him. 'Don't get your hopes up, Josh. It doesn't happen very often and you're only here until Friday. Some of those items have been hidden away for years. One day I'll have to admit to myself that it's a waste of time keeping them any longer.'

'No, don't put them in the auction!'

Clive laughed at me. 'You have to face facts, many lost things are never returned to their owners, no matter how much they're loved.'

I didn't want to hear that and for the rest of the day each time a customer came to the counter I hoped the enquiry would be about a precious item and that I would be able to find it for them.

I've lost an umbrella, last week on the 6.13 from Katoomba. Black, wooden handle.

A Britney Spears beach bag.

A tan leather wallet with the initials GRV embossed in gold.

Most of the enquiries were like these, but if it was something the least bit out of the ordinary – a cake tin, a hot water bottle – I went after it like a bloodhound. There were no ladies in search of a family heirloom and certainly no nervous, unshaven men seeking their diary, though that didn't matter. That Monday was still a buzz.

My vigil continued on Tuesday, and afterwards I went to the movies with Alicia, Melanie Stewart and a bunch of their friends.

'Hey, what's this about a party for your band on Friday?' Melanie asked in front of us both. 'Neven Vanderoy says you two were supposed to invite us.'

I'd told Alicia about the party but I hadn't passed on the general invitation. She looked at me quizzically while I explained, giving the lame excuse that I'd been too busy working. When she got me alone later she wanted the truth.

'I thought it would be better if it was just us. None of your eagle-eyed friends around. More private, you know, for you and me.'

When she finally understood what I was getting at, her face became serious. Any second now she was going to deny everything she'd hinted at on New Year's Eve. Before she could say a word, I tugged her close to me, holding her tenderly as I'd done under the trees in the Domain and whispered, 'Hey, it'll be like New Year's but without the grass and the chance of anyone watching from the trees.'

She snuggled against me to show it was all right. The warmth and the softness of her body sent a thrill through me and if it hadn't been for the movie theatre, garish and noisy around us, I could have believed it was Friday night and we were already alone in a bedroom, somewhere in Dave's house.

Alicia's mother drove us home and we held hands in the back seat like a pair of Year Eights. The TV was off in the family room when I walked in, which surprised me. Hayley was supposed to go to bed at nine, but all through the holidays she'd stretched her luck whenever she could. Oh well, Dad must be laying down the law tonight.

But Hayley wasn't in her own bed, she was sitting on mine, her knees up to her chin, arms wrapped around her long legs.

'What's up?' I asked from the doorway.

'Where have you been!'

'Out with Alicia.'

'You should have been here, Josh.'

'Why, what happened?'

'Mum was crying again.' The effort of telling me was enough to make Hayley sob as well.

I hurried to slip my arm around her and sit beside her on the bed. 'Did Michael ring again, was that it?'

My sister's head shook from side to side, words were too difficult. After a few seconds to let her get a grip, I dropped my voice to a whisper. 'Did she shout at Dad like last time?'

'No, just crying,' she managed to say, fighting for the words. 'It started after tea when we were doing the washing-up. Dad couldn't stop her. He tried, but he couldn't and she didn't want him to come near her. It was awful, Josh. I don't want them to be like this.'

'Neither do I.' She let me guide her into her own room where I finally left her reading with the light on over her bed. No point trying to make her sleep when she was so stirred up. The light was out in Mum and Dad's bedroom and I assumed Dad was in there, so it was a shock to discover him in the dark-ened living room, just sitting there silently, like a shadow.

'Sorry, Josh. I didn't hear you come in,' he said, standing

to switch on the light. His eyes blinked in the sudden brightness.

'Hayley said that Mum was . . . upset.'

'Hayley,' he whispered with a start, as though he had left her at the beach and only just remembered.

'It's okay. She's in her bedroom, reading.'

He brushed past me, on the way to her room anyway, and I could pick out the deep murmur of his voice through the wall. By the time he left her I was back in my own room, with the door closed for no particular reason. Tonight it just seemed that each of us was condemned to shut ourselves off – Mum in her bedroom, Dad out there alone in the darkened house, and Hayley and me in our own little bolt-holes.

It was a relief to join Clive in the Lost Property Office on Wednesday morning. Who could tell, today might be the day a customer came looking for something special. The hours dragged, though, the phone so quiet I checked it twice for a dial tone.

'Do you mind if I have another look through that suitcase?' I asked.

Clive didn't look very keen, but he shrugged and let me bring it out to the round table. The old Bible had only ever been an obstacle to my exploration on earlier visits to the suitcase, but this time I opened the leather cover for a closer look.

'It's eighty years old,' I noted, reading the fine print below the title. On the opposite page a simple list of names had been written in pairs, with dates noted beside them.

'Birth dates,' said Clive, peering over my shoulder. 'First name, second name, date of birth. It's an old tradition in some families. There's four generations recorded in there.'

The need to handle these things, to know them and guess what they might mean to the men and women who had lost them grew as quickly as I could feed it. There wasn't a lot in the suitcase, though, and I was soon left only with the photographs. I worked the elastic band over the end of the bundle of envelopes and opened the first. Say cheese. Every second photo was of smiling kids, someone's daughter, son, grandson, grand-daughter. Our albums at home were the same, mostly of Michael, Hayley and me, growing our way up the measuring stick of Mum or Dad.

The smiles were different from face to face, though. I began guessing the personality of individuals, inventing what I couldn't work out and wondering where they were now. In the second set a bunch of guys not much younger than me were goofing off for the camera, on their way to the Easter Show. On the train they had tried to chat up some girls who featured in the photos, smiling in a bemused kind of way at first, then growing uncomfortable, even angry, as the photographer kept clicking away and his mates sat beside them, making faces. Pricks.

I browsed through the other sets during my lunch break and during the flat spot in mid-afternoon, but there are only so many photos of nameless, smiling faces you can look at. By five, the bundles were back in the suitcase and the suitcase snug behind the pram in the last bay of the compactus. Only the boredom of Thursday morning sent me back to them again. Even then, the first set brought the same glaze to my eyes. Please, somebody, come down the ramp and tell Josh Tambling of the precious thing you've lost.

No luck, though, so I continued through the holiday snaps of Mum, Dad and four kids, deciding this would be the last. At least there was a story here, sketched out in the pictures: Sydney Airport, a gleaming tour bus with them all standing near the door and then a dozen shots taken from a boat with a string of islands in the hazy background.

'Great Barrier Reef,' I murmured.

After their day on the boat, they had gathered on the dock for a couple of final shots, all in the classic pose, taller ones at the back, squirts at the front. I was ready to toss these last few onto the pile and take them all back to the suitcase when my hand froze.

This picture was badly taken, cutting off half of the mother on one side and leaving a big gap on the other, which meant the camera had snapped as much of the scene beside them as the family. That was what had caught my eye. An unshaven, weary-looking guy was standing beside a blue plastic crate with fish tails spilling over the side. Not that I really saw the fish at all. I was only interested in the face. The guy was side-on to the camera, but his profile was enough. It was Michael.

'Clive, Clive!' I shouted through the Lost Property Office.

He hurried towards me, frowning. 'What's the matter?' When he saw no one at the counter, he raised his eyebrows, ducking his head deep between his shoulders in a puzzled shrug.

'It's my brother Michael. He's in this photo!' I blurted out, shoving the picture in his face.

'Steady on, Josh. Your brother. Just a coincidence. No need to go berserk.'

'No, you don't understand. I've never told you about my brother. He's missing. Won't tell Mum and Dad where he is.'

Clive took the photograph from my hand while I bounced around nervously beside him, wanting him to see it but desperate to snatch it away again.

'There,' I insisted, stabbing at the picture with my index finger.

'The bloke with no shoes on, looking down at the fish?'

'Yes, him. Where is it, Clive? Do you recognise anything in the picture?'

He gave me an exasperated glance and didn't answer. My heart sank. 'How am I going to find out where the picture was taken?'

'There's a boat in the background,' he muttered, but we couldn't read the name and panic took hold of me. To be teased this way with a glimpse of Michael, but not be able to do anything about it . . .

'Wait a minute. Where are the rest of the photos, Josh?' He picked the bundle up off the counter and started through them.

'What are you looking for?' I demanded when progress

seemed agonisingly slow. 'They are up on the Great Barrier Reef. You can see that.'

'Yes, but the Reef's a thousand miles long,' he muttered and kept at his detective work. 'Ah, this is what we're looking for.'

I craned my neck over his shoulder and found him examining the shot of a busy shopping street.

'Nope, nothing to help us in that one.'

The next was no use either, but in the third we struck gold. 'Angelo's Seafood,' he read from a sign. 'What does it say underneath that, Josh?' he asked, handing the picture up to me.

I focused on the sign, but the smaller letters were barely legible. At least we could guess some of it from the seafood connection. 'Best Fish and Chips in . . .'

What followed was the name of a town, I was certain, but which town? 'Six letters,' I told Clive, 'and the last one's a "y". Damn, the first letter would be more useful, but I just can't make it out.'

'Six letters, a "y" at the end. Could it be Mackay?'

'Yes, yes, that's it,' I cried. 'Michael's in Mackay!'

'Well, he was when that picture was taken,' said Clive, dampening my excitement – and he had a point, too. The photo could have been taken more than a year ago. But when your luck is in, it's really in. The photograph had the date printed in the bottom left-hand corner – September last year! A little over three months ago.

I had to tell Mum and Dad.

Mum's number diverted to her voice mail and it didn't seem right to give such momentous news to a recording. Besides, I wanted to hear Mum's surprise, the gasp of air, I wanted to share the excitement.

'Mum, it's Josh. Call me as soon as you can.'

Then I rang Dad. After three rings there was his voice, alive and listening.

'Dad, it's me, Josh.'

'I've got a client with me, Josh. Can I call you back?'

'No, Dad, it's too important. I know where Michael is!'

Silence. I don't know how long it lasted, only a couple of seconds maybe, but I was bursting with the news and I couldn't wait. 'Did you hear what I said, Dad? Michael. I've seen this photograph, taken just a few months ago. I've worked it out . . . well, Clive and I have worked out where it was taken. I know where Michael's living.'

Then Dad's voice cut across mine. 'Mackay. Michael is living in Mackay.'

Silence again; my silence this time. 'You know already,' I managed to say at last.

'Yes, Josh. He was in Mackay early last year and as far as I know, he's still there.'

'But how . . . ?' That was just the first of a hundred questions colliding in my head like a pile-up on the freeway.

'Have you told your mother?'

'No, she's not answering her phone.'

'Then don't tell her, Josh. Please.'

'But Dad, what's going on?'

'I'll explain tonight, Josh. Please do what I ask and I'll see you at home.'

He had said 'please' twice. He hadn't made me promise or demanded that I give my word not to tell Mum. Just said 'please'.

'What happened?' Clive asked when I put down the phone. He hadn't been listening in, but he could obviously tell that the calls hadn't gone as I'd hoped.

I tried to straighten my face, but the effort was too much and I just waved a hand at him and turned away.

'Here, under the circumstances, I think you need this photo more than the people in it,' said Clive. I took it from him and slipped it into my pocket without really knowing what I was doing.

Dad had known where Michael was for a year. What was going on?

chapter fifteen

Dad was home when I arrived, which didn't surprise me. It didn't surprise me either that he was hanging around in the kitchen, waiting for me.

'I didn't get your message until late, Josh,' said Mum, 'and by the time I tried the Lost Property Office, there was no answer. What did you want, anyway?'

Dad stiffened and his eyes locked onto mine. I had never been in this position before. It was always *me* who looked to *him* for help. He was the strong one who could make things right with a few words or something as simple as picking me up when I was hurt and crying.

'I needed a lift around to Alicia's. Doesn't matter now 'cause I'm not going.'

'Is that all? You sounded pretty excited.'

'No, nothing exciting. Just Alicia's place.'

Mum still didn't have a clue. She took down a saucepan from the rack above the stove. 'Since you're home early,

Phil, could you pick Hayley up from squad training?'

'Of course. What about you, Josh?' Dad asked as he pulled the keys from his pocket. 'You want to come for the ride?'

I hadn't heard those words in quite a while but this wouldn't be like all those rides years ago. He set off towards the garage without waiting for a reply. Before the Statesman was even out of the driveway, I was after answers. 'How did you know Michael was in Mackay?'

'Private detective.'

'Are you serious!'

He nodded without apology as he turned his head to check for traffic. 'It wasn't difficult, apparently. Michael is using his real name. I got the news last February.'

'So why haven't you gone up to Mackay?'

''Cause it would look like we were hounding him and that would only make matters worse.'

'Why did you go to all that trouble if you weren't going to do something when you found him?'

'To know he was okay. I had the detective watch him long enough to be sure he's not doing any drugs. He's safe, Josh.'

'But that was nearly a year ago!'

Dad had to wait for a couple of cars at the end of our street before touching the accelerator lightly so that I barely felt the pressure of my back against the seat. He was just as cautious with his reply. 'The investigator said he seemed settled, overheard him talking to people in a pub, that he liked Mackay and was planning to hang around. Then there's his phone calls. You can tell better than me, Josh, does he sound safe?'

'Shit, Dad, Michael's a bullshit artist! He could tell me anything and I wouldn't know if it was true.'

'But he doesn't sound sorry for himself, does he? He's defiant, laughing at us.'

'What does that prove? The times he stood up to you most at home was when he was drunk.' I was almost shouting. Almost! No, I *was* shouting.

Dad kept his eyes on the road, didn't even flinch. Damn. He just didn't get it. I took the photograph from my pocket and, when he stopped the car at a red light, shoved it in front of the steering wheel. 'He doesn't look so great in that. He's begging for a bloody fish to feed himself.'

Dad stared at the picture until the light turned green. Said nothing.

'I can't understand why you don't go up there and talk to him, tell him it's all right to come home.'

'Would it be all right though, Josh, or would we end up like we were before he left?'

He was taking everything so calmly, as though he had already been over it a hundred times. To me, it sounded like defeat.

'Dad, why did you ask Michael to leave?'

He checked the rear-view mirror and turned the airconditioning down a notch. Took a breath. 'Lots of reasons, Josh. Your mother, mostly, she was walking around the house like a shell-shocked marine waiting for the next explosion. The doctor already had her on antidepressants.'

'She didn't want Michael to go, though.'

Even though we were doing eighty ks on the main road, he closed his eyes and replied softly, 'No, she didn't. That was my decision.'

That's the end of it, he's not going to discuss this with me any more, I thought, but when he opened his eyes again, he said, 'I thought about getting him a job on a cattle station out west somewhere. It would have been more like a working holiday and a break for your mum, too. I could have swung it, you know. I've got dozens of graziers on my books.'

'Didn't Michael want to go?'

'Never had a chance to ask him because your mother vetoed the idea. She said it was like admitting we'd failed him. She's always worried about that, Josh, that her mother's love wasn't strong enough, that the way things were such a mess for Michael was her fault. There was no way she was going to let him move so far away from us.'

'Well, he's a long way away now,' I retorted, knowing how cruel the words would sound. I didn't care, I wanted them to hurt.

'I had to make him leave, Josh. I thought he'd kick around Sydney where we could keep an eye on him. We didn't ever think that he would go off on his own and not let us know where he was.'

'Or those phone calls?'

'No, not that either.'

'Do you think he knows how much they drive Mum crazy?'

'He wants them to hurt, yes, but Michael's not malicious. Every time he calls he's reminding your mum and me how he's cut us out of his life. But he keeps ringing, Josh, as a way of saying, "Stuff you, Dad." If he didn't care about us, if he really wanted to cut us out of his life, he wouldn't ring at all.'

Dad guided the Statesman into the car park beside the pool. Hayley wouldn't be too long because on the other side of the cyclone wire the swimmers were all out of the water and gathered round the coach.

'I *hate* those calls,' I said with more emotion than I had ever put into a song. 'I hate being the one in the middle.'

Dad stared at me, startled. 'I'm sorry, Josh, I never thought . . .'

'You know what the worst thing is? He never listens to me. He doesn't know how I hate it.' There were tears on my cheeks now, stupid, treacherous tears that I slapped away.

'It's all right, Josh.' Dad's hand stretched towards me, almost touching my arm before I pulled it away.

'I get so angry at him. I just want to yell into the phone and tell him not to call any more. But I can't, he has to keep calling.'

A few kids appeared through the gates. Cars were starting up. Hayley would be here any second.

'What are you going to do about Michael?' I asked.

'What can I do, Josh? Michael's biggest problem is me, who I am, everything he knows about me. None of that's going to change. All we can do is hold firm, keep everything together . . . and trust Michael.'

Trust Michael! I wanted to argue with him all over again but here was Hayley picking her way quickly across the loose

136

gravel with a towel around her waist. Even after five kilometres in the water she was still in a hurry.

'What's for dinner? I'm starving,' she demanded as the door closed and Dad joined the queue of cars waiting to turn onto the road.

Neither of us answered until Dad realised she was waiting with a quizzical frown. 'Oh, um, sausages and mashed potatoes, I think.'

They were the only words spoken on the way home. By then Hayley's frown had deepened into a scowl. After Dad went into the house ahead of us, she tugged at my elbow.

'Are you in trouble, or something?' she whispered, more out of sympathy than suspicion.

I wasn't in the mood for sympathy. I pushed her hand away savagely. 'No, everything's fine.'

But everything wasn't fine. It was mucked up big time and now I'd let my little sister cop my angry confusion. The frightened look she gave me as she squeezed past almost stopped my heart. 'Not you too, Josh. Not you and Dad.'

I should have called her back and told her what was going on. I should have marched into the house and told Mum where Michael was. I should have, should have, should have . . . but I didn't.

Dave rang early on Friday before I'd left for work. 'How did you get on, talking to Alicia?' he asked, coming straight to the point.

'Yes, she's coming and so's Melanie Stewart and maybe one

or two others.' I couldn't resist a dig. 'Who knows, Dave, you might get lucky.'

'Not likely,' he said with the lazy lack of resolve that blighted the guy's entire life. I was ashamed of goading him about the girls now. Dave would be stoked if one just sat and talked to him for ten minutes.

'Has Gemma rounded up any of her girlfriends?' I asked.

'No. Hasn't said if she's coming herself yet.'

That was a surprise. 'Why not?'

'Search me! One minute she's making love to Neven's guitar and the next she's playing hard to get. He doesn't know what's going on. Anyway, if you're speaking to any more girls . . .'

'Yeah, I get the message. See you tonight, Dave.'

By that Friday morning, I had to face facts: there wasn't going to be any miracle. Come on, let's get real here. Clive kept those sentimental items hidden away on the off-chance that some-one just *might* turn up one day and ask about them. Even he seemed to have a time limit. My time ran out at five p.m. that afternoon.

About noon, I went out to get some lunch from the kiosk at the far end of the concourse. Washing my hands in the toi-let afterwards, I spotted a condom vending machine reflected in the mirror. I'd never dared more than a glance at the lurid pictures on the front before, but today I hung around, a self-conscious sweat under my armpits. What the hell, no one was watching. The coins were ready in my fingers.

You're kidding yourself, Tambling. Nothing's going to happen tonight.

My fist closed over the coins and I turned towards the door. No, nothing was going to happen, but I went back and fed two dollars into the slot, just in case.

Back in the office, my uneasiness grew until my mind was crowded with more worries than it could handle. Mum and Dad and Michael, and poor Hayley, and the way the guys dissed my singing, not to mention Dave's party tonight and the slim packet tucked into my shorts. There were others I couldn't quite name but to stop and count every ball I was juggling would bring them all crashing down. I was suddenly terrified that if I let that happen, then Josh Tambling would shatter into a night sky of countless stars and far-away galaxies.

The image left me breathless and sweating and when Clive called, 'Josh, there's someone here to see you,' my first thought was to hide in the compactus.

Get a grip, Josh, I raged at myself. Who was it, though? Clive's stout figure obscured my view. Michael, was it Michael? This was a stupid hope, I knew, but my mind was steering its own course today. I moved quickly to peek around Clive just as a familiar voice said, 'Hi, Josh!'

'Gemma! What are you doing here?'

The surprise in my voice chased the easy smile from her face. 'I hope it's all right. I was in town, you see, and I thought that I'd . . .' Her words trailed away as though she was suddenly sorry that she'd come at all. 'I'm not getting you into trouble, am I?'

'No, no, it's fine. Too bad you didn't come a little earlier. I've just come back from lunch.'

Clive solved that problem. 'It's quiet as a church in here today, Josh. Go on, take another break. As long as you like. It's your last day, after all.'

'Let's go up to the kiosk then,' I said, leading her up the curved ramp and onto the concourse.

'It is okay to visit you like this, isn't it?' That was the second time she had asked, as though she was nervous about coming to see me.

'Not much point in firing me. I finish in a couple of hours, anyway,' I assured her. 'Hey, I'll buy you lunch, if you like.'

'You don't need to do that. I can pay.'

'I'm rolling in it right now. Been working at this place for four weeks and the money's just piling up in the bank, mostly.'

'That's because you're not a girl with a wardrobe to fill,' she shot back with a grin.

'Is that why you're in town?'

She looked at me blankly for a moment then came to life, 'Oh, er, well yes, it is actually.'

She must have been heading up to George Street later because she wasn't carrying any shopping bags. We found a table at the kiosk and I bought Gemma a hamburger and a milkshake.

'How's Alicia?' she asked.

'She's okay.'

'Are you taking her to Dave's party tonight?'

I shrugged. Having one girl ask you about another wasn't the easiest of conversations, especially when my feelings towards the two in question were so out of kilter. I wanted Gemma to help me forget this morning's worries. Instead, she was adding to them.

'You don't look very happy about it,' she said tentatively.

'Don't I? Better get my act together then.'

'Like New Year's Eve,' she said and immediately seemed to regret it when I stared at her in surprise.

'What do you mean about New Year's Eve?'

A tinge of pink flushed her cheeks. 'Sorry. I didn't mean to pry, but I was watching you.'

'I was watching you, too, with Neven.'

She hesitated, looking down at her hands before tossing her head back with a wry smile. 'Yeah, Neven. He's a lot of fun.'

The talk about Alicia and Neven felt like another jab in my ribs and on top of so much else on my mind I almost had to close my eyes to keep focused. Before I knew it, Gemma was talking again. 'He wants me to go to Dave's party with him.'

'Who?' I had to ask because I had somehow lost the thread of what she was on about.

'Neven, of course.'

'Oh, sorry.' I didn't want to hear about Neven and Gemma getting together and I couldn't understand why she was telling me.

After another awkward pause, she asked, 'Did you really watch me on New Year's Eve, Josh?'

The expression on her face was suddenly serious. I started

to panic. Maybe I had said it the wrong way just now, made it sound like I was a voyeur peeping on her and Neven. I backtracked hastily. 'Not really. I just saw you kissing at midnight and I thought, hey, love the one you're with.'

Incredibly, she seemed disappointed when I said that. Sometimes chicks are impossible to read. I gave up trying to make conversation, in the hope that Gemma would change the subject.

'Josh, you know it was a funny thing, that night in the Domain. Even with the bands blowing our eardrums out, I still picked out the stars and remembered the things you told me.'

'You don't agree with me,' I noted in a noncommittal tone. Though I was relieved she was no longer talking about Neven. Or Alicia.

'No I don't, but there were other things you asked me, about what difference it made to me; believing in a God, I mean. Like, did it make me do anything differently.'

'You said you just acted out of who you are. I thought that was a fair enough answer.'

'Well, that's just it. I've been thinking about your question ever since because if it didn't make any difference, then there's not really much point to it all.'

'So what's your answer now?'

'Oh damn, now I have to explain it,' she said, laughing at her own reluctance. 'How do I say this without sounding like those fruit cakes on Sunday morning TV.' She hesitated again, one eye on me, obviously hoping that I would let her off the hook. No way. Gemma was the only person I'd ever spoken to about these things. I trusted what she thought and though it was weird to be talking like this in the middle of the noisy concourse, I was desperate to hear what she had to say.

'He's in the back of my mind, all the time, I think. It's how I judge whether something is good.'

'Like right and wrong, you mean?'

'Yeah, that, I suppose,' she said cautiously, the hesitancy in her voice sounding as though she was still not sure how to explain.

'Religions don't have a monopoly on judging right from wrong,' I said bitterly. I'd worked that much out in Study of Religion classes. I should have stopped there, but it was a bugbear of mine that I'd fumed over, sitting in church beside Dad, and so I had to add, 'Oh, they claim it all right, but mostly they are just trying to make rules to suit their own view of the world.'

Gemma leant forward so she could rest her hand on my arm, and said softly, 'No, Josh, I didn't explain it properly. Forget right and wrong. I was talking about things being good. More important than that, it's how I know that I'm a good person. If I didn't have a sense of God in my head, I'd lose that.'

'A good person,' I said with a cynical laugh. 'Is that what it's about?'

Gemma's mobile rang. As she fished it out of her cute little shoulder bag, I was distracted by the sight of a woman thread-ing her way through the tables behind Gemma. I was sure it was Mum. Gemma glanced down at the screen to read the number.

'It's Neven,' she said, looking up at me.

What would Mum be doing here? I almost jumped to my feet and called out to her but just in time, the woman turned a little more my way and I saw it wasn't Mum at all. Of course it wasn't: she was at work. I sat back in my chair aware that my heart was beating double-time and that across the table, Gemma was asking me something. I'd missed it the first time so she tried again.

'Should I answer it, Josh?'

Why was she asking me? Shit, there was so much crammed inside my head, it's a wonder I wasn't bleeding from the ears. When I didn't respond, she pressed a button and put the mobile to her ear. 'Hi, Neven.'

chapter sixteen

Gemma looked as though she was settling in for a lengthy chat to Neven so I made signs that I had to go. She smiled beautifully at me and blew a kiss without breaking stride in her conversation. Chicks are amazing the way they can do that.

'Nice girlfriend you have there,' Clive teased when I let myself in through the 'Staff Only' door.

'Girlfriend!' I replied with a snort and at the same time thinking, *I wish*, but to Clive I said, 'That was Gemma, just a friend I talk to a bit.'

About three o'clock, Dad rang to say he was going to be in town later and did I want a lift home?

I said 'no', straight away, and stood there afterwards with the phone in my hand wondering why I preferred a dreary train ride to sitting in the airconditioned Statesman beside my father. The question became tangled in a mess of thoughts that sprouted every which way inside my muddled mind. What was wrong with me today?

Then it was five o'clock and Clive closed the safe, collected his plastic lunch box from the fridge and slipped it inside his tattered backpack along with the thermos.

'Well, it's time to say goodbye,' he said and he shook my hand as he had done on the first day. 'I've enjoyed having you work here with me. I hope you'll drop by and say hello if you're passing through the station.'

'I'm sorry about the auction,' I started to say, but he swept it aside.

'Proves you're honest, doesn't it. You'll do all right, Josh. Good luck with those exams at the end of the year, eh?' and he let go of my hand.

All afternoon I had been making up little speeches in my head, trying to find the right words of farewell. I could thank Clive for being a good boss but that wasn't what I wanted to say. Gemma's visit was still in my mind, especially what she had said about believing and how it was something to measure herself by. If I wanted to thank Clive for anything, it was for being a good man. But how did I do it, how could those words ever come out? I didn't know and now the moment had passed.

Clive ushered me out through the door one last time and we set off towards the platforms until we reached the point where our paths diverged. Around us the impersonal echoes of the huge terminal went on indifferently, the distant rattling of baggage trolleys, the scuffing of shoes on the hard stone floor, the cry of a child.

'Don't forget, if you find any lost property, even the small things can be valuable. You know that now, I guess. Goodbye Josh,' he said and, with a wave, he stepped into the crowd and almost immediately became invisible.

I moved off down the escalator and joined the wave of bodies that swirled and surged and buffeted its way along the tunnel towards my own platform, where I was finally cast adrift and more alone than I had ever felt in my entire life.

A train rattled and screeched to a halt in front of me; my fellow passengers swept aboard, but not me. If I got on this train, then the week was over and I couldn't bear that. There was more to it with Clive, more he had to tell me. If I was quick, maybe . . . I hurled myself back up the escalator and into the tunnel, struggling against the human tide this time and earning angry glares from the people I collided with. Then up the stairs for the Strathfield Line just in time to make out the tail lights of a train receding into the spaghetti of tracks towards Redfern.

Left behind, lost.

No not lost. Don't be ridiculous. I knew where I was, who I was. Josh Tambling, from Oatley, Phil's son, you know, the famous footballer. Time to go home, now, to where my mum was doing homemade pizza like she'd done every Friday night since Michael had pronounced it the best pizza in the universe.

It was only ten past five. Plenty of time for that. I walked out onto Eddy Street and down to George. The sun was still strong wherever the skyscrapers couldn't hide it and the shops were open, drawing bodies in from the pavement and spitting others out. I stood outside Planet Hollywood listening to the music and bought a medium fries at the McDonald's next door. Then I drifted towards the harbour, gazing through the plate-glass windows at lifeless mannequins, at books standing open on piles of themselves and strings of pearls with thousand dollar price tags. Passing a pharmacy I winced involuntarily and wondered why until I remembered the condom in my pocket.

I kept walking and looking at the people, and found myself wondering whether they had lost anything, whether any of these faces had ever turned up at the Lost Property Office in search of something more precious than any price Mr Witworth could get for it.

The fading light didn't register with me until it was almost dark. I was sitting on a bench in Hyde Park by then, watching a jogger circumnavigate the grounds for the third time – going in circles, like me. I should be at home, but there Michael's absence hung in the air, making a permanent night-time that leeched the life from my family.

No, I had to go. Alicia would be waiting for me to take her to the party. Oh shit, the party, with Dave's parents gone for the night and the possibilities in my pocket.

I crossed Elizabeth Street against the lights and made it to Town Hall station. Only three passengers shared the carriage with me as it rattled and swayed through the ink-black night, where street lights pretended to be stars and the planet's atmosphere reeked of a Sydney summer's day. Each of us was our own universe, until the woman three rows ahead of me tried to open the narrow window above her seat. It wouldn't budge, so I moved into the row behind her and yanked the window open.

'Oh, thank you. We need all the breeze we can get tonight, don't you think?' and she returned to her seat. But as I backed into the aisle to do the same, my leg brushed a plastic shopping bag.

'Is this yours?' I asked the woman.

She had to swivel awkwardly and peer over the back of her seat to see what I was pointing at. 'No, not mine.'

Someone had left it there then. I bent closer and started to go through it.

'Careful, might be a bomb,' said a man from the rear of the carriage, chuckling to himself.

The bag held two empty soft-drink cans and the screwed-up wrapper from a Cadbury's Flake, but that bag of rubbish started me off. I looked around the rest of the carriage.

'What are you after, mate?' the same voice called out, minus the sarcasm this time. 'Have you lost something?'

'No, not me.'

I knelt down and scanned under the seats. Nothing. There was nothing in any of the empty rows either. When I passed the third passenger, a woman close to the doors, she clutched her handbag to her side and deliberately avoided eye contact. The fool! I didn't want her handbag, I wanted what people had left behind.

There was no joy in this carriage but at the next station I

stepped out onto the platform and into the carriage behind where I quickly found a baseball cap with a smudged name inside, *Jodie*, and a phone number. That was a start, but it wasn't what I was looking for. Another stop, another carriage, this one a dud as well.

The next stop was Oatley. My home. Mum and Dad would be wondering where I was, and Alicia was waiting. The doors opened. The hard concrete of the platform met my feet. The cleaner, cooler air of the suburbs touched my skin. Time to go home.

I walked towards the overhead bridge, passing the unsearched carriages. The speakers above my head blared, 'Stand clear please. Doors closing,' and when they closed, I was back inside the train.

Those last three carriages shouldn't take long. The job would be done by the time we reached Sutherland and there were trains going by all the time. I'd be back at Oatley in twenty minutes, thirty max.

But on board the citybound train, I set to work again. These carriages allowed movement between them, so I searched methodically, starting with the first where I discovered another plastic bag, this one with a damp towel and a pair of boys' board shorts rolled inside. I added Jodie's cap to the swimming gear and kept going, slipping into a routine, the upper floor of the split carriage first, beginning with a slow walk along the aisle, checking left and right and at the end I'd drop to my knees and look under the seats.

There were passengers on board, of course, though I barely

noticed them until a guy called out, loud enough for the whole carriage to hear, 'He's lost his marbles, eh? Have any of you seen them?'

His friend looked down frantically, lifting his feet, 'Haven't rolled under my seat.'

Yeah, good one. They were still laughing when I moved on to the next carriage. Later, a man watched me go through my routine and asked, politely this time, 'What are you doing?'

'Collecting lost property.'

'What have you found?'

'Nothing, really. Not yet, but you never know, you see . . .'

How could I explain about the brooch and that crazy guy's diary or the Italian love letter? The guy would have to work in the Lost Property Office, like I did, to understand what it could mean to people.

The train was well past Oatley by the time I reached the last carriage. From Hurstville it had become an express to Redfern so there was nothing I could do but sit by the window as the train barrelled through Kogarah, Rockdale, Banksia, the familiar names of my childhood, and all too fast for me to catch hold.

I couldn't go home now, I argued with myself, it was too late. Even though I knew they'd be waiting – Mum, Dad, Dave, Alicia – I was gripped by a compulsion to keep on searching, convinced that there was still stuff to be found on these trains.

I took the first train that pulled into Redfern, heading for Bankstown, but I was on my way back again soon enough, with a beach umbrella and a John Grisham novel added to my hoard. At Sydenham I transferred to another Illawarra Line train and had it thoroughly searched by Penshurst. There was a comfort in all this searching. I didn't have to think while I was on my hands and knees. Best of all, there was the hope of what I might find and the pleasure it would give me.

It was taking forever for a train back towards the city to arrive and when another southbound one cruised in, I thought, what does it matter which train I'm on? Any one of them could have the special thing I was looking for on board. I searched until a mumbled announcement from the driver called over the loudspeaker, 'Cronulla, Cronulla Station. This train terminates here. All passengers must leave the train.'

I stepped out into the evening with seven or eight others who all scurried away immediately, their footsteps mingling with the dull swoosh of a solitary car's tyres. Then I was alone on the platform, except for the flagman who was walking the length of the train, checking through the windows for anyone who had fallen asleep.

'How long till the next train into the city?' I asked him.

'There's no more trains tonight. First one's at five-thirty in the morning.'

'Five-thirty!'

'Sorry. What'd you do? Fall asleep and miss your stop?'

'No, I didn't miss it, I . . . There's got to be another train.'

'Not tonight,' he insisted, stepping aboard, and seconds later the warning buzzer sounded, the doors along the full length of the train drew together in perfect unison and the train shunted away slowly to wherever it slept the night.

No more trains. It didn't matter that I was stranded so far from Oatley; more the hard reality that there was nothing more for me to search. I sat on a bench surrounded by the things I had recovered from the carriages, the loose handles of the plastic bag rustling in the ocean breeze. This was all I had to show for my searching, a yellow and blue striped beach umbrella, two books, the protective case from a mobile phone, plus Jodie's cap and the damp swimming gear.

My shoulders slumped and, closing my eyes, I leaned back against the cold aluminium of the seat. Every moment I remained still on the platform took me further from what I had been doing on the trains. My body's needs began to return, as though I had somehow ceased to be human these last few hours. I went to the edge of the garden bed and pissed torrentially onto the flowers. Back on the seat, I saw, at last, how pathetic my collection of lost property really was. None of it was worthy of Clive's suitcase, to be held in secret trust for the peculiar people who might, just might, have a desperate need for what they had lost. I pushed the bag away from me and fell forward, burying my head in my hands. What had happened to me tonight? Where had the hours gone between leaving Central Station and arriving here at Cronulla?

My skull felt like the clockwork model Kepler built to explain the heavens. Clive and Mum and Alicia were all planets trundling awkwardly on concentric steel rings around me at the centre. My own gravity was dragging them in towards a spectacular collision, a Big Bang, and for a moment I was aware of myself in the universe: a tiny speck under a light on a deserted railway platform, isolated and alone, with no maker and no meaning, just a body with lungs that kept breathing and a heart that kept pumping and most of all a brain that wouldn't stop, couldn't stop, thinking.

'Hello, Dad. It's me, Josh,' I said into the payphone I'd found in the mall opposite the station. All the shops were closed and the sea breeze gusted papers along the deserted street like tumbleweeds. I might have been the caretaker of a ghost town. Maybe I was the ghost.

'Josh, where are you? We've been worried sick. It's one o'clock in the morning.'

I apologised meekly and told him where to pick me up. He must have burned up the road because the Statesman pulled in at the end of the mall fifteen minutes later.

'Are you all right?' was his first question when I climbed in. 'No one's been after you. No one tried to . . .'

'No, nothing like that, Dad. I just lost track of time.'

'That's bullshit, Josh. You don't lose track of time for eight hours!'

I clammed up and let him get through the angry bit – and he *was* angry all right. 'Alicia was worried too. She called three times looking for you. You were supposed to take her to a party.'

'I'm sorry,' I muttered as though Alicia was there in the back seat. Shit, I still had the condom in my pocket. I would have to keep it out of sight until I could get rid of it.

'You'd better ring her in the morning just to let her know you're all right. She sounded as worried as we were. And as for your mother . . . it was bloody inconsiderate of you, Josh, when you know damned well what else she's been dealing with.'

Guilt stuck me in the ribs big time when he said this. I didn't want to make things any harder for Mum than they already were. 'I'm sorry,' I said again, sounding like a mindless chorus. I'm sorry, I'm sorry, I'm sorry. But there was no relief in the words, no absolution, none of the release that comes with admitting what you have done wrong. I might as well have still been sitting on the platform back there at Cronulla.

At home Mum hugged me and told me off in the same breath. Anything else she had been about to say disappeared when she suddenly grabbed at my wrists.

'Look at your hands! Josh, what have you been doing?'

Instinctively, my eyes dropped to inspect my open palms. Gross! All that crawling around on the floor of carriages had left them filthy.

'How did they get into such a state?' Mum demanded.

'We were moving stuff at the Lost Property Office, cleaning shelves, a lot of dust,' I lied quickly.

They glared at me doubtfully through weary, bewildered eyes, but neither had the stomach for more. 'Get in the shower and clean yourself up,' Dad growled.

Glad of the chance to escape, I obeyed immediately and emerging with only a towel around me five minutes later, slipped straight into my room. The light went out in the hall soon after and the door of their bedroom clicked closed.

Reaching the safety of my room was one thing, sleep was another. I lay on my back looking up at the darkened ceiling. What the hell had I been doing tonight? Though Dad didn't believe me, the night *had* become timeless, as though every tick of the clock had been sucked into emptiness, taking me and my pathetic collection of lost property with it, into a private universe.

Enough of that. I was sick of the stars and the questions they posed. I wanted answers, I wanted to find what I had been looking for tonight, or at least work out what I had lost.

Ghosts and fear stalk darkened bedrooms when sleep won't come so I almost fell out of bed in fright when the door opened and a figure took two tentative steps towards me. 'Josh, are you awake?'

'Shit, Hayley, you nearly gave me a heart attack.'

She froze, the silhouette of her shoulders hunched unhappily. 'Can I come in?' she whispered. It was more a plea.

'Yeah, close the door and I'll put my reading lamp on.'

My sister slept in red shorts and a white T-shirt, always the same ones, making sure Mum washed and dried them so they'd be ready. I'd never asked her why before. 'Is the red and white for St George?' Hayley went to more games with Dad than I did last winter.

'What? Oh, my pyjamas. Yes, I suppose.'

I wedged my pillow against the wall and sat up, making room for her to sit beside my legs.

'Where did you go tonight?' she asked breathlessly as she sank onto the mattress. 'I was so worried.'

'You've been awake all this time?'

She nodded. 'I thought you'd run away too.'

Run away! Her words sounded like bad American television. 'Kids run away in the Brady Bunch, Hayles. That's not what happened with Michael.'

'I don't know what happened with Michael. All I know is that he's not here and tonight I thought you were gone too. You're not going to go, are you, Josh?' She grabbed my hand as though this would hold me prisoner in my room.

It hadn't occurred to me until then how much this whole mess was getting to my sister. For all the noise she made around the house, she was still like Dad when it came to the deeper things. She kept them to herself, only letting them out when she was desperate and afraid.

'I'm not going anywhere, that's a promise.'

She relaxed her grip on my hand after that. Just as well because it was cutting off the circulation in my fingers. 'I wish Michael would just come home,' she muttered miserably.

'So do I, Hayles, so do I,' I repeated with an honesty that left me desolate.

Her head bobbed up, catching the full glow from my reading lamp. Her eyes were dry, which surprised me. Perhaps she was like me – tears came with anger and frustration, not from misery.

'I don't think Dad knows what to do, Josh. He looks scared,

don't you think? Scared for Mum, scared he won't be able to make it right like he always does.'

This was so like my own thinking that for a moment it hurt to breathe. I opened my mouth to tell her that Dad already knew where Michael was but wouldn't do anything about it. At the last second I held back. 'He said we have to trust Michael, that he will come home one day.'

Hayley didn't react to this the way I had done. 'Mum doesn't think he'll ever come home. I heard her talking to Dad tonight. She thinks we've lost him for good.'

'Lost him!'

Hayley stared into my face, a hint of confusion, even fear in her eyes. 'What is it, Josh?'

'Uh,' I grunted, not really listening to her. *Lost him.* I had been searching for lost items all night, but I had never been going to find what I was looking for, any more than one of Clive's lucky customers was going to turn up at the counter this week. And all that time the thing I was searching for was one of the things I was trying to forget about.

Already my mind was planning what to do, because I knew what I had to find now and an exhilaration was taking over, driving out the loathing and the misery of those minutes on Cronulla Station. Could I pull it off? Did I dare?

'Are you okay to sleep now?' I whispered to Hayley as gently as I could because impatience was threatening to burst out of my chest. When she nodded, I got out of bed and led her back down the hall. 'I'm glad you came to talk to me tonight. Try not to worry about Mum. Once Michael comes back she'll be okay and, you never know, he might be back sooner than you think.'

Back in my room, I could barely wait for the morning. Yes, I knew what I had to find now and better still, where to find it. I'd get on that bus with Dave and Tom tomorrow, but I wouldn't get off with them at Port Macquarie. I had a lot further to go, all the way to Mackay.

n the morning, I lay in bed planning the trip and how to find Michael on the streets of Mackay once I'd arrived. I'd have to ask around, and the picture Clive had let me keep wasn't much use. Time to find a better one. The albums in the living room were too precious to raid so it would have to be a snap from the mess of loose photos in the bottom of Dad's filing cabinet. Ten minutes of searching turned up a picture of my brother scowling at the camera. Would it do? Depended on how much he'd changed since it was taken.

'What are you looking for?' a voice asked over my shoulder.

I jumped so suddenly that poor Mum staggered backwards a step.

'I wanted a picture of Michael for my room,' I lied.

Mum seemed touched by this, adding to my pangs of guilt. She took the picture from my hand. 'Not a very good one, but

I doubt you'll find much better. He flatly refused to stand in pictures with the rest of us once he left school.'

So this one would be pretty old. I did the calculation in my head until the figure I came up with surprised me. Back on my feet, I looked down at her and said, 'Mum, most guys Michael's age would have left home by now anyway, don't you think? Is it really such a big deal that he's gone?'

'It's not that he's gone, it's the way he went,' she replied quickly. 'I feel cheated. It's not the way I wanted to let him go.'

She gave me back the photograph and I decided it would have to do. But as I slipped it into my pocket I wondered whether Michael had grown any older in Mum's mind than he was in that snapshot.

When Mum came back from shopping just after lunch, she drove me to the bus station in Eddy Street, only metres from where I had worked for the past four weeks.

The guys were pretty stunned when I told them. 'Mackay! What are you going up there for?' Dave demanded.

'My brother Michael's there. I've got to find him and bring him back home, before Mum cracks up altogether,' I explained.

They stood with me in the line while I waited to change my ticket. 'But what about all the things we planned? What about the chicks?'

Ah, trust Dave to get right to the heart of any issue. 'You'll have to pull your own chicks, Dave. Wear a bag over your head when you go down to the beach and let them fall for your body instead.'

That earned me a thump on the shoulder. I had already apologised for missing his party and received a detailed report of his failed attempts to crack onto every girl who showed up.

'Alicia was there looking for you,' Dave confided, dropping his voice to little more than a whisper. 'You're in trouble there, mate. She had a face like an axe murderer.'

Oh shit! I should have phoned Alicia this morning before I left, but there were calls to make about schedules and I could only do that when Mum took her radar ears to Coles. I'd ring from a stop along the way.

It was only after Dave and Tom left the bus at Port Macquarie about sundown that I was truly on my way. I had spent some of the time juggling figures in my head: $240 for the ticket to Mackay and the same to get back, though I hadn't booked a ticket yet because I wasn't sure of the date. If things went as I hoped I would need two tickets, anyway, and there was plenty in my bank account to cover that. Even after deducting the bus fares, I still had a thousand dollars for whatever might be needed to get Michael home.

I hoped he was all right. There was only so much I could bluff my way through and if I had to take him to a hospital or a social worker, they would want names and explanations. I'd bring him back, though, if he was still there and I could find him. What could be more precious – what could have greater sentimental value to my family than Michael? This was going to be so good. Roll on, bus, I cried in my head.

My iPod and a Matthew Reilly thriller helped to while away the hours. All around me passengers began settling down for the night. Sleeping in a bus seat wasn't so hard, especially next to the window. By the time the sun speared a wakening jab into my eyes it was already past five o'clock and the bus was chewing up the freeway between the Gold Coast and Brisbane.

The connection to Mackay left at a quarter to eight, giving me an hour and a half in the wild excitement of Brisbane's Transit Centre. It was lousy with stale cigarette smoke and weary travellers like me. I'd never been in Brissie before; I could have a look around, maybe get something for breakfast. Slipping my ticket into a deep thigh pocket along with the iPod, I headed out into the morning air. A footbridge over one wide road led to an outdoor escalator, which I rode down to a sign saying George Street. I might never have left Sydney!

There wasn't much to see in Brisbane's George Street this early on a Sunday morning. I bought a sticky-bun and bottle of OJ at a café and by a quarter to seven I was carrying them back towards the Transit Centre, pretty much done with Brisbane.

I crossed at the lights, passing two guys a little older than me on my way to the escalator. They followed me aboard so I shifted to the left in case they wanted to get past. One of them did, though once he was a step ahead of me he saw that his mate wasn't in such a hurry and he moved to the left in front of me.

With such a close view of his back, I couldn't help noticing the Stüssy shorts, like mine, with a hole torn in the back of one leg. The Nike runners were new but the gap at the heels showed he could have done better with the fit. His big brother's maybe.

At the critical moment when you have to transfer your weight from the moving step to solid ground, the guy dropped a coin. He dived down onto his hands and knees trying to rescue it. Before I could react, I fell over the top of him, my head on one side of him, my legs on the other and my arse pointing at the sky.

'Oh, sorry, mate,' I said automatically, though it was his fault. He was back on his feet while I tried to collect my breakfast and the book that had spilled out of my hands. 'Well, did you get your ten cents back, at least?' I asked, looking up at him.

He didn't answer, didn't apologise or offer me a hand. He was already backing away, looking over his shoulder towards his mate. Then the pair of them took off like rabbits across the overhead bridge and down a ramp leading into the street below.

What was going on? It was all a freakish accident, wasn't it? Why were they running . . . Oh shit! I reached for the back pocket of my shorts. My wallet was gone.

'Hey, you bastards,' I shouted and took off after them. They saw me coming and switched their three-quarter jog into a full sprint along the footpath. A woman in church clothes and a man with his coat slung casually over one shoulder were walking the same way. By the time I called out, the thieving mongrels were past them. A long line of cars waited at the traffic lights, but the faces inside did nothing more than gawk at us.

I had narrowed their lead to thirty metres by the time they cut round a sharp corner and headed uphill towards a park. 'Drop my wallet!' I yelled. Fat chance of that. They crossed the road and attacked a set of grey stone stairs that led into the park. I was quickly onto those same stairs and climbing, my lungs ready to burst by this time.

Then, bang! The next few seconds were a complete blank, as though the tape of my life had been wiped. Where it begins again, I was kissing the rough asphalt of the path and my lungs were heaving desperately. Dust caught in the back of my throat, making me cough, but feeling was coming back into my body. For some reason my cheek was on fire. My left hand dragged itself round to touch it gingerly – ouch! – while I tried pushing up onto my knees. That was when one of the bastards kicked me in the ribs.

'Quit chasing us, ya dickhead,' a panting voice commanded, then they ran off.

Time didn't run in the usual way after that, so how long I lay there groaning is anyone's guess. By the time the first passer-by stopped to inspect me, I was looking around to see exactly where I was.

'Are you all right?' said an old guy in shorts and long socks.

'You tell me,' I said.

'Well, you've cut your face.'

I tried again with my hand, which came away with flecks of blood on the fingers.

'What happened?' he asked.

'I was running and they must have . . .' Any more and I was announcing a crime. Best to shut up.

'Should I call an ambulance? You've gone very pale.'

'No, no, I'll be fine.'

He went off doubtfully. If I didn't want every Good Samaritan to give me the same attention, I realised I had better get out of the way.

Ouch again. The pain wasn't from my face so much, but my ribs where the mongrel had kicked me. I made it to a park bench and rested there for a while. Every breath hurt, but it was no more than a dull ache as long as I stayed still. A woman leading two balls of fur on a leash eyed me off suspiciously, but didn't stop.

The world was coming back to me slowly. I was in Brisbane, in a park looking out over the high-rise. In fact, I was above a big railway station and just beyond it was an ugly building that seemed made entirely of black glass. There was the bus station, too, I could even see McCafferty's buses parked on a concrete apron.

It was a slow walk back. Some of the early morning strollers gave me a wary look as I wiped away the blood. The cut was about an inch from my left eye and already the area all round it was swelling as though a balloon was being born though the side of my face. The Transit Centre promised a kind of safety. I fell into the first plastic chair I came to. Oh shit, my ribs hurt. I touched my shirt where the oversized Nikes had made contact but didn't dare explore the damage. The bastards had punched me in the face then kicked me while I was on the ground. How low was that! Anger burned across my skin, bringing a clammy sweat that doused the fire and left me sobbing instead at a picture of myself at their mercy.

What was I going to do? I was a thousand kilometres from home, my parents didn't know I was here and they would be furious when they found out – furious with me! Phone, public phone, phone card. No, forget it, those two mongrels took my wallet! Painfully, I dug around in my pockets, but besides my bus ticket and the iPod, the search yielded just the fifteen cents change from the sticky-bun. It would have to be 1800 REVERSE.

There was a Telstra booth across the concourse, but with my finger poised over the numbers, I worried again about what would happen when I told them. Dad has footy friends everywhere. Most likely, he would ring one of them who lived in Brisbane and ask him to come and get me. In the meantime, Dad would fly up here himself; maybe Mum as well. It was going to be ugly – and their anger was the easy part. They'd want an explanation and Dad would go ballistic when I told him about Mackay. Worse than that, much worse, Mum would want to know why I was heading to Mackay in the first place and then the shit would really fly.

I looked down at the keypad again and started to dial the numbers. Mum answered in three rings.

'It's me,' I told her as brightly as I could. 'Just ringing to let you know that we made it here to Port Macquarie okay. Yeah, Dave's sister is nice. I'll ring again in a day or two.'

Somewhere in there had been a decision, though don't ask me exactly how it was made. My ticket would still get me to Mackay, to where my brother was living and once I'd found him I'd worry about how to get us both home again.

The large digital clock at the end of the concourse showed 7.38. There was still time. I headed for the elevators to get me up to the floor where the bus would be waiting because there was no way I could manage the stairs right now.

To hide my injured cheek from the bus driver I developed a permanent need to rub my forehead with the fingers of my left hand. My seat was on the aisle, which meant no leaning against the window to sleep as I'd done last night.

'Any chance of a swap?' I said to the woman who was already in the seat beside mine.

'I asked for the window especially.'

She'd spotted my cheek and didn't like what she saw and those narrow eyes didn't miss the smudge of dirt on my shirt, either. To her it was more evidence of my scruffiness; to me it was the bullseye of my pain.

The way she was looking down her nose needled me. I wanted to say, 'Hey, my dad's a famous footballer, he drives a Statesman, we live in a nice house.' But these things weren't doing me much good at the moment, were they? So I kept my mouth shut.

The woman huddled against the window and didn't say a word all the way to Bundaberg. Not that I wanted a conversation. I was light-headed and dozy for a couple of hours and a dull nausea settled into my guts. Just as well since my breakfast was crow food back in Brisbane and my only cash amounted to fifteen cents.

The geography of Queensland's coastline is not my forte but I learned one thing on that bus – it's a bloody long way between the dots on the map. Each time we stopped, I hoped my grim-faced companion would get off, but she remained doggedly in place, heading all the way to Cairns, most likely. Night closed in during the dinner break at Gladstone and after that the highway became an isolated ribbon through unrelieved blackness. The dizziness had become a thumping headache and my ribs mocked the idea of a comfortable way to sit, yet soon after we left Gladstone my body simply shut down and I slept.

'Hey, matey, wake up, it's time to get off.'

I opened my good eye to darkness and a shadowy figure beside me. The eerie silence meant the bus had stopped. 'What's the matter?'

'Nothing, we're just in Mackay, that's all. Come on, I'll get your bag out from under the bus.'

Gaining my feet in the aisle was a struggle but I managed somehow and followed the driver to the door and down the steps into a fug of tropical air.

'It's dark,' I said, disoriented. 'The timetable said quarter past one.'

'That's right. We're spot on time, too.'

Except that I'd assumed that *1.15* meant the afternoon, not the early hours of the morning. The driver hauled out my bag and left it at the kerb for me to fetch. Then she was straight back into her seat, pressed a button to close the door and that was that. I had arrived in Mackay.

The McCafferty's Office was closed. In fact, the entire town was closed. I couldn't start searching for Michael until the morning, anyway. Where to now, then? With money in my pocket, I would have tried for a room at the motel across the road. Yeah, with money in my pocket. Those mongrels in Brisbane!

Just stooping to grab the handles of my bag warned me what to expect: my ribs weren't going to let me get far with this weight. Gritting my teeth, I carried, dragged, kicked my bag as far as the next corner. There was a park not far away but even from here the silhouette of the palm trees and the open spaces around them seemed too exposed to sleep in. I kept walking, somehow carrying my bag in the hope of something better, but after a hundred metres the pain was too much. A driveway led between two houses to a block of units behind. This would have to do. At least it was out of sight from the road. I settled on a patch of grass between a parked car and a rickety fence, using my bag for a pillow and, despite the relentless agony of my ribs, fell asleep again within seconds.

chapter eighteen

'Wake up, come on, get moving. You're not sleeping off any hangovers here, sonny boy.'

For the second time within hours, I struggled up through confusion and debilitating lethargy, forcing myself awake. This voice was aggressive, like a guard dog with a human tongue. I sat up and immediately groaned deep in my throat.

'And don't go throwing up here, either, or I'll make you clean up the mess.'

A short, beefy man in a white singlet and football shorts stood in front of me. The keys in his hand said he was the owner of the car I had slept beside. At least it was daylight. A glance at my watch told me it was after seven.

'Piss off, you filthy bastard,' he continued and when I didn't scramble instantly to my feet he sent a half-hearted kick towards my outstretched legs, missing by a metre.

'All right, all right, I'm going.' I got up awkwardly and lifted the bag over my shoulder. The pain was razor sharp and startling behind my eyes. I almost blacked-out and had to double over to get the blood back into my head.

In daylight, the street turned out to be an odd jumble of houses and offices. Just short of the corner a waist-high brick fence penned in two wheelie bins with *Regional Eco Industries* painted on the side. Between the last bin and the side fence was a narrow gap hidden from the front door and invisible from the street unless you were looking for it. I slipped through the iron gate and deposited my bag in the darkened space.

Wait, the iPod. I'd slipped it into the bag while I slept, but decided to keep it with me now just in case. There were two more things I needed today as well: photographs – the one Clive had let me keep and the one from Dad's filing cabinet. As for the rest, I'd be back for the bag when I was ready. The important thing now was to find my brother.

No building in Mackay seemed much higher than two storeys. The centre of town was set out in a grid pattern so I had no problem working my way along palm-tree lined footpaths into the main streets where milk bars and bakeries were beginning to open. I showed Michael's picture to the shop assistants.

'Sorry, mate, don't remember seeing the guy.'

'No, doesn't look familiar.'

'Geez, what have you done to your face?'

That last response was the most common. People wouldn't concentrate on the photo because they were too busy staring at me. A few turned away in fright, sometimes mingled with impatience. 'I got a business to run. You buying anything?'

Outside one shop where the rotted awning left a gap, I caught sight of my sunlit face in the window and understood why. What a mess! My left cheek was swollen like a tennis ball, crowding my eye, which explained the constricted view on that side. It hadn't bothered me much until I saw my reflection. Under my eye the skin was the maroon of a Queenslander's football jersey.

Only eight-thirty and already the languid heat was taking hold of me like a fist. As if it wasn't hard enough to breathe already! But worse than the heat was the hunger. My last meal had been on Saturday night, thirty-six hours ago and yesterday's nausea was long gone. My stomach was demanding an explanation; no, stuff the explanation, it wanted action. For an hour, I did my best to ignore it and kept showing Michael's picture to anyone who would stop in the street.

About ten o'clock, I stumbled across the police station but if I asked about Michael in there, they would want to know about my injuries. I'd leave them as a last resort, I decided, but the sight of the police station set me thinking about other official places.

'Centrelink,' I said out loud, earning a quizzical look from passers-by. Michael was probably registered for unemployment benefits. Why hadn't I gone there first?

But no one recognised his face at Centrelink.

'His name is Michael Tambling,' I explained. 'You could check on your computer to see if he's listed.'

The guy behind the counter looked as though I'd stuck a gun in his face. 'Can't do that. Privacy laws.'

No one had seen my brother at the St Vincent de Paul thrift shop either.

'Look, he might be sleeping rough. Where do . . . you know, the homeless, I suppose, where do they go in Mackay?'

'Not much of a problem here,' a woman told me, fidgeting with a price tag in self-conscious concern. 'If you like, I could ring our local branch. They'll get you a meal and a place to sleep.'

Me! I escaped into the humid street, so completely without energy now that one foot would barely push itself ahead of the other.

This was stupid. What the hell was I doing? A one-man search party, a starving search party at that, with fifteen cents in my pocket. I should ring Dad – get it over with. I forced myself along the street. Was I looking for a phone booth? Maybe. What I saw instead was a sign in a shop window, *Cash for Anything*. My hand felt for the iPod and before I could change my mind, I walked inside.

At first glance, I might have been back in the Lost Property Office, though here the jewellery was on display in glass cabinets. Fishing rods, surfboards, flutes and guitars, they were all here. IPods, too, I noticed eagerly: a couple with hundred-dollar price tags.

The store was one of a nationwide chain that advertised at home, with cheerful young attendants offering a fan of fifty-dollar notes for all sorts of junk. Greeting me in this store was a man older than Dad with eyes like little brown beads that caught the harsh light from the street.

'Do you have proof of purchase for the iPod?' he asked.

'No, I'm away from home, you see, and . . .'

'ID then?'

I shook my head.

'Twenty dollars,' he said.

'Twenty! It's almost new. You've got much older models out there for a hundred dollars.'

'No proof of purchase, no identification. How do I know you haven't stolen this?'

'Bullshit. It's mine. Look, I wouldn't be selling it except that . . .' I started to explain about the robbery in Brisbane but the swelling on my cheek marked me as desperate and the more I told him the more he knew he could screw me.

'Twenty dollars is all I can offer you,' he repeated.

'Get stuffed!'

The clock set into the side of an explorer's monument in the centre of town clicked up to midday. Lunchtime in Mackay. Every café, every fish and chip shop, every deli was pumping out aromas that tantalised me. Hunger is so immediate. It comes around every five or six hours or so, and you have to feed it. If you don't, it starts to eat you.

Outside a McDonald's, my feet took command of my head. Not that I could afford a single thing on the menu but maybe I'd find some chips left behind on a table, or the dregs of a milkshake. With one eye out for staff, I circulated among the tables. Nothing, and as soon as anyone got up to leave, an eager fourteen-year-old swooped onto the tray. I could have killed him. Instead, I lowered myself gingerly into a chair to enjoy the delicious torment of so many smells.

Macca's is Macca's no matter where you are. Does the scene even need a description? A mother argued with her three young brats about what to order. A handful of teenage boys, younger than me but dressed much the same, huddled in three separate groups. Two girls sat opposite one another exchanging furtive secrets. The prettier one had dark hair to her shoulders and smooth, tanned skin, reminding me of Gemma.

The place was almost silent until three older guys burst through the doors. Their accents identified them as English – backpackers most likely. They ordered at the counter then sat down close to me. It didn't take long for them to spot the girls.

'Ah, tropical hotties,' one commented to the others, making no effort to keep his voice down.

'Birds of paradise,' said a second. This was a game they'd played before.

'Hey, sweetheart, give us a smile,' called one of backpackers, speaking openly to the girls now.

Both turned their way without thinking and this little victory encouraged the guys. 'How are ya, darlin'?' said the same backpacker, exaggerating his accent. 'Waiting for your lover boys, are you?'

The girls pretended not to hear.

'They've stood you up. Come over here and sit with us instead.'

It wasn't just the girls' attention they had captured. All heads swivelled their way now, even the staff. Whispers were exchanged behind the counter until a striped shirt went off purposefully through a side door just as one of the girls let the Englishmen know what she thought of them.

'Pigs,' she hissed.

After a triumphant glance between the three of them, the guys stooped low over their trays, grunting noisily. The girls made for the door, bristling with disgust and indignation. As soon as they were gone, the backpackers rushed to the window to watch their victims stride away in fury and slapping themselves on the shoulder as though their football team had won the FA Cup.

That was when the manager arrived, a skinny bloke no older than they were but he was armed with authority and he wasn't taking any backward steps. 'Gentlemen, you are harassing customers. You'll have to leave.'

One of the backpackers started to argue, though his mates were tired of the joke and sounded more conciliatory. Not that I paid much attention because while this was going on, their meals lay half-eaten on the table beside me. Everyone was watching the show. No one was watching the table.

I was so hungry.

No, I couldn't. What if they caught me? But my stomach was shouting louder than my fear so with one eye on the circus at the window and ignoring my ribs as best I could, I snatched up a hamburger and made for the door.

Nothing ever tasted so good.

It was the exhilaration of what I had done as much as the food that kept me going through the afternoon until I'd been into every store and asked half the shoppers of Mackay whether they'd seen my brother. All for nothing. Not a single spark of recognition. My ribs ached in time with the beats of my heart, my feet were sick of walking, the heat had drained the energy from my body and my stomach was letting me know that half a hamburger was no substitute for the meals it had missed.

Looking up and down the street, I saw the river and took myself there to rest for a while on a wall overlooking the bank. Low tide exposed ugly, glistening mud at the river's edge and the bank of the other side seemed to melt into mangroves. A large white bird, an egret or a crane, flapped low over the grey-blue water, aimless and alone, it seemed to me.

This is hopeless, a voice despaired inside my head. Michael might not even be in Mackay. He's moved on to Darwin or somewhere. I can't go on scavenging for food. I need money in my pocket to keep searching. Without actually admitting what I was going to do, I tugged the iPod from my belt and headed towards that sign, *Cash for Anything*.

The cheapest meal in Mackay was two dollars' worth of chips at Jeff and Leslie's Take Away. Everywhere else has a two-dollar fifty minimum serve and forget Macca's because you don't get as much potato for your money. I spent the first two dollars before I even thought of a supermarket instead. There, I checked things out for tomorrow and found that a litre of milk was $1.85 and a loaf of bread cost $2.35. Various combinations played around in my head. I hadn't done so much mental arithmetic since primary school. At two meals a day, averaging two dollars a time, I could last for five days on the twenty dollars the mongrel gave me for my iPod. I still burned with the humiliation of it, but the thing was, I could keep searching.

The sun was going down, my bag was a kilometre away and I couldn't carry it anyway. Best to leave it hidden. I went back to the river where I'd spotted a likely place a few hundred metres downstream from the bridge. Out of sight of the road, I tried to get my ribs comfortable. Nothing seemed to work, not lying on my back, not on my good side. Sleep wouldn't come. An hour after dark the mozzies swarmed around me but I was too exhausted to find anywhere else. The hope that had flared briefly in me after the chips now washed away with the tide. Slapping at the invisible hordes, I slept rough for the second night. Above me the cloudless sky opened onto the universe as it always did. But I had other things to think about that night. There was no time to worry about what it all meant while my body was giving me this much grief. My last thoughts were of a comfortable bed in Oatley, and of Mum and Dad and Hayley and, if I could only find him, Michael, too. For now, this was the full extent of my universe.

At least Tuesday morning didn't start with shouting and a kick at my legs, which was just as well because my chest and back were so stiff now that it took a few minutes just to stand up. By the river, the temperature had dropped in the early hours and my shirt and pants were damp with dew. I stood shivering until I realised that I was being watched after all. A fisherman stared at me from thirty metres away, his rod wedged against his stomach. My path back to the road took me within a couple of metres of him.

'G'day,' he called, smiling, or was he laughing at me? He was about Dad's age but nowhere near as fit, judging by the belly that anchored his rod. 'Been here all night, have you? Jesus, the mozzies have had a go at you.'

I looked at my arms and legs and saw that I had been scratching them, without noticing, since I woke up.

'Looks like you've had a run-in with more than mozzies, too.'

'I'm all right,' I assured him half-heartedly. I took the photographs from my pocket and showed him the better one of Michael. 'You haven't seen this guy lately, have you?'

He shook his head immediately. 'Sorry.' But he saw the second picture in my hand. 'Is that another picture of him?'

'Sort of.'

He took it from me. 'I can help you with this one, though.'

'But you said you hadn't seen him.'

'Not your mate, no, but I can tell you where this picture was taken. Out at the marina.' He pointed at a detail in the photograph. 'That's the new rock wall they built as a breakwater. Look, I'm going home that way if you want a lift.'

Why not. It was worth a try. I didn't realise until his battered Falcon had crossed the bridge and we were quickly eating up a lot of road that this marina was so far out of town.

'About five kilometres, maybe six,' he told me when I asked.

He dropped me in a parking lot and drove off with a cheerful wave, his fishing rod protruding through the rear window. Maybe this wasn't such a good idea, after all, but I was here now. When I emerged from between the parked cars I found myself high above a glittering marina protected from the sea by the massive breakwater of loose grey stone that the fisherman had seemed so proud of. Five low jetties, walkways really, poked out from the shore like the teeth of a giant's comb. The gleaming reef cruiser I'd seen in Clive's photos was moored at the side of the widest jetty, opposite two fishing trawlers.

Cautiously, and using the handrail like a pensioner, I made my way down a long flight of stairs and out onto the jetty. For no particular reason, I held the picture out in front of me and lined up the familiar landmarks to find the exact spot where it had been taken. There, got it. I was standing right where the photographer had been when he'd snapped Michael in the background.

But Michael wasn't there. Of course he wasn't. This picture was taken four months ago and people didn't stay frozen in one place for four months, just because their photo had been taken. He might have only come out here once, hoping to snaffle a meal. Seemed a long way to come just to beg, and didn't I know that. I had to get myself back into town if I wanted to keep up my search.

I shuffled back along the jetty, my only companions a pair of curious seagulls eager for scraps. 'Don't look at me,' I scowled at them. 'I had to scavenge my own breakfast yesterday.'

My unhappy legs got me as far as the stairs when a man's voice started up behind me, coming rapidly closer. I glanced back to see a guy in grubby overalls chatting on his mobile as he strode along the wharf, following the same path I'd covered so laboriously. He would pass me any moment, heading up the stairs. His phone call ended just in time for me to ask, 'Are you going into town by any chance? I could do with a lift.'

'Sorry, mate. Got work to do here yet.' He nodded behind him towards one of the trawlers.

Without thinking, I raised my arm in a 'no worries' gesture but my ribs paid a price for that.

'Are you all right?' the man asked when I staggered sideways clutching at my chest.

'Yeah, yeah, I'm fine,' I assured him but when I straightened up, he was studying me with a frown. Judging by the first signs of grey hair over his ears, he was about forty, not exactly tall, but strong as an ox and his hands were leathery and thick-fingered, like wicket-keeping gloves.

'What are you doing out here, anyway? You don't look too flash. Were you looking for something?'

Was I still looking for something? In the last couple of minutes had I quietly decided to give up and call Dad instead. When I didn't answer immediately, the man continued up the stairs, taking two steps at a time.

'No, wait,' I called. 'I'm looking for someone who maybe hangs around here sometimes.' I held the two photos in my hand still but the stairs seemed too much to climb. I started to describe Michael instead. 'He's about my height and quite muscly, though he might not be so strong these days, like he hasn't been eating properly. He's twenty-two, no, twenty-three,' I corrected myself quickly. What else could I say about my brother? What did I know about him? 'He talks a lot and he can be pretty funny sometimes.'

The man looked down at me as though I was the funny one; not the kind of funny that makes you laugh, either. 'Does this bloke have a name?'

'Name? Yes, his name is Michael Tambling.'

'Mike Tambling! Yeah, I know Mike.'

The excitement built so quickly I forgot the agony in my ribs and climbed the stairs to show him the photograph.

'That's him,' the man confirmed.

Was this really happening? 'I'm trying to find him. Can you tell me where he is? Like, does he have a place where he sleeps or anything?'

'I don't know the address exactly, but I've got his phone number.'

Address! Phone number! This was getting more unbelievable by the second.

The man was inspecting me closely now that I'd come up with a name he knew. 'Listen, you don't look in any condition to go finding anyone right now. I'll call Mike and see what he wants to do.'

He completed his journey to the top of the stairs, punching numbers into his mobile as we went. By the time I joined him he was speaking animatedly into the phone. Spotting me, he dropped the phone away from his ear and said, 'Mike wants to know who you are and why you're asking about him.'

'Tell him it's Josh. I'm his brother.'

He repeated my words, listened for a few moments, then

with a simple, 'Sure, okay,' he cut the call. 'He's coming to get you,' he called to me. 'Be about fifteen minutes. Do you want a drink of water or something?'

Coming to get me. Fifteen minutes. Was that it? This had to be a dream. Maybe I was still asleep on the river bank, but when the man brought his water cooler from the trawler, a larger version of Clive's thermos, it seemed real enough. I downed the icy water in one gulp and held out the white plastic mug for another. Three more cupfuls of that wonderful water had chilled my throat by the time an old Commodore came round a bend and revved towards us, pulling into the nearest vacant parking slot. The wheels had barely stopped before the driver's door burst open and out stepped my brother, Michael.

chapter nineteen

'Josh, it *is* you!' Michael called as he came towards me.

How had I described him to the man from the trawler? Muscular, but maybe not doing so well. I was wrong about that, very wrong. Michael was wearing tattered grey Stubbies and a singlet in no better condition, but the arms and shoulders and thighs that stuck out of them were toned and sun-tanned and glistening under a sheen of tropical perspiration. He looked fit enough to jump into the ring with Mike Tyson! As he came closer I saw fine crow's-feet of un-tanned skin in the creases at the corners of his eyes. He'd been out in the sun a lot, no doubt about that. His face was more open than I had ever seen it, inviting a smile or a word of 'hello' and there was something about his walk that the cheap pair of thongs on his feet couldn't disguise.

He was close enough to see my cheek now. 'Jesus, what happened to your face?' he cried, signalling with his hand towards his own. 'Look at it!' he breathed in mock awe, coming even closer and ducking his head a little for a closer inspection. 'Don't tell me, I should see the other guy, is that it?' and he laughed at his own joke.

'I had an accident, tripped over when I was in Brisbane.'

'Yeah, sure. Fell into a door, right.'

'Broken concrete on the footpath,' I lied. 'It's no big deal.'

Michael stood back for another look at me. 'I can't believe it. Shit, you've grown, mate. I was expecting a little squirt like you were last time I saw you.'

Had I grown that much since he left home? Suppose I had.

'I'd better introduce you two properly, eh? This is my boss, Trevor Mills, Trev to all his mates. Trev, this is my little brother, Josh.' As he said brother, he slapped his powerful arm around my shoulders and tugged me in close.

My ribs felt like they were going to spear out through the skin of my chest. Before I could stop myself, I broke away from him and doubled over, groaning and swearing under my breath.

'What's the matter, Josh? Jeez, I didn't mean to hurt you.'

'No, it's okay. My ribs are a bit sore from sitting up so long in the bus.'

'Sitting up in a bus! Bullshit. Let me have a look under your shirt.'

Trevor was concerned as well. He stepped closer and helped me raise my shirt high enough for Michael to have a look.

'Holy shit! It's worse than your face,' gasped Michael, inspecting the massive crimson stain painted across the left side of my chest. 'This didn't come from an accident,' Michael said sternly. 'Tell me the truth, Josh. You've been in a fight.'

'Look, it's nothing to worry about. I got mugged in Brisbane, that's all.'

They asked me more about the robbery and I answered as best I could, growing more miserable with every pathetic word of explanation.

'I don't like the look of these ribs, Trev. What do you reckon, the hospital?'

'Yeah, get 'em X-rayed for sure.'

'That's what I was thinking. Better take him now, but I'll have to ring Kel first.'

'Here,' Trevor said easily, handing over his mobile.

Michael walked off a couple of metres, facing out to sea while he made the call. That left me with his companion, who started to lead me slowly towards the Commodore. 'You've come up to join Mike, have you? Looking to work on the trawlers too, eh?'

The trawlers? I looked again at the pair of boats moored one behind the other opposite the cruiser. 'Are you really his boss?'

'Yep, that's my trawler, there, the *Jeannie Mills*. Named it after me mother. Mike's been with me for a year now. He learned the ropes real quick. Wouldn't be without him these days.' He turned away from admiring his own boat and strode on beside me to the passenger's door. 'Tell you what, if you can work half as well as your brother, I might consider taking you on one day.'

I mumbled something about being at school. No one had ever held Michael up as a model for me to emulate before. Unless Trevor was being sarcastic, and he didn't strike me as the sarcastic kind. He helped me into the car just as Michael jogged up, his thongs flapping rhythmically in time with his steps. 'Let's get you up to emergency and sort you out, eh?'

We were barely around the corner from the wharf when Michael started on another matter, one I had been waiting for. 'Look, Josh, I didn't want to say anything in front of Trev, but how the hell did you know I was up here? More to the point, does Dad know?'

Much of those first hours alone on the bus had been spent wondering how I would answer this. Of course Dad knew Michael was in Mackay, but he hadn't come up here to see his son and he might have been right about one thing: if Michael knew the truth, he might take off again. Then things would be back at square one.

'No, Mum and Dad don't know anything about this.' It wasn't entirely a lie, after all. I fished around painfully in the pocket of my shorts for the photograph. 'Dad got me a job at the Lost Property Office. There's this amazing old guy who runs the place and . . .' It would take ten minutes to explain about Clive while all Michael wanted was to have his fears allayed. 'There were all these sets of photographs that I was going through and I found this one, taken on the wharf back there.'

Michael took the picture from my hand and held it close to the steering wheel where he could inspect it while still keeping one eye on the road. 'That's me,' he said, surprised. 'We must have been unloading fish by the look of it. How did you know it was taken in Mackay?'

I explained as briefly as I could.

'And you didn't tell Mum and Dad. You came up here to see me yourself, instead. Josh, you're a legend,' he laughed, dropping the photograph into my lap and reaching out suddenly to tousle my hair, the way he used to when I was so much shorter than him.

'Thanks, Josh. Not just for coming up here to see me. That's great, but for not telling them, especially. I'm not ready yet, okay?' He took a breath and hugged the wheel closer before saying the same thing again, softly, seriously, 'I'm not ready.'

Michael found a park close to the emergency ward without any trouble. The sun was like a laser on my neck and arms even for that short walk to the doors. A nurse took my details and a doctor came out to assess my condition soon afterwards. 'Great collection of mozzie bites. You want to watch out for Dengue Fever,' she commented. 'As for those ribs, we'll need a closer look.'

We waited half an hour for the X-ray results and another half an hour before the doctor was free.

'Okay now, let's see,' said the doc as she slid the large sheets of dark film out of their envelope. I was lying on fresh sheets in a curtained-off cubicle by this time, with Michael standing anxiously beside the bed.

The doctor read the brief written report, checking the

X-ray against the ceiling light a couple of times. 'There,' she said, tapping the film with her forefinger.

Michael squinted to see what she was pointing at. 'Broken?' he asked.

'Yes, two of them. There's no treatment except rest, but I can give you something for the pain. Do your ribs hurt?'

'Only when he sees a pretty girl,' said Michael, trying to flirt with the doctor who ignored him in a good-natured way and looked at me for an answer.

I didn't feel like being the hero. 'Yeah, they do a bit.'

'I'm not surprised. The ribs and your face, too. Just as well you've got your brother here to take care of you.' She helped me sit up on the bed first of all, and then stand, gripping my arm tightly when I became light-headed. Bending over a desk in the corner of the cubicle, she wrote out a prescription. 'Careful with these pain-killers. They're stronger than anything you can buy over the counter,' she warned, handing the folded prescription and the envelope of X-rays to Michael before a parting instruction. 'And don't go lifting anything heavy for at least two months.'

Lifting anything. My bag! I told Michael about it as soon as we were through the curtain and back in the waiting room.

'I thought you were travelling a bit light. Come on, we'll get you those pills and then go find it.'

The bag wasn't there. We checked down the side of the building and Michael even went inside to ask.

'Not having much luck, are you, Josh? Where did you sleep?'

I led him back along the street and down the laneway to the block of units. A vindictive part of me hoped my tormentor of yesterday morning would come down to investigate. Michael would sort him out, big-time. No sign of him, though, or the car I had slept beside.

'You were taking a risk,' my brother commented, 'but I tell you what, I slept in worse places before I lobbed here.'

'Like where? All those calls you made, where were you?'

He grimaced and turned his head aside as though the question was too much. 'Does it matter, Josh? Come on, I'll take you home.'

Home! Oh, how I wished he could simply drive me a few blocks and drop me outside our house in Oatley. But Michael meant *his* home, of course, and after ten minutes through the streets of Mackay he turned into the driveway of a low-set house with a flat roof and fibro sides. The second driveway at the other end and two front doors separated by a lattice-work screen confused me at first.

'It's a duplex,' Michael explained. This half is ours. Couple of harmless old ducks have the other half.'

The front yard wasn't much to speak of, but someone had cut the grass not long ago and a massive bougainvillea clung to Michael's side of the house, crowning the tiny front porch with a headdress of deep pink.

While Michael was helping me out of the car, the front door opened. Sudden movements were not a good idea at the moment so a few seconds passed before I saw who had come out to greet us. From beneath the shady arch of the bougainvillea a young woman stared back at me. The narrowness of her face was emphasised by the long straight hair that fell on either side and down her back, but to be honest that wasn't what caught my attention in those first few moments. Her dress, made of lightweight cotton and almost see-through, stretched down to her ankles. Around her shoulders and legs it was loose fitting to combat the heat but in the middle, her stomach pushed outward in a huge bulge that took up every centimetre of space the dress allowed.

'Josh, this is Kelly,' said my brother once we had mounted the three steps to the porch. To the young woman, he said, 'Don't worry, he looks better without a black-eye. Had a little accident, but he's fine now.'

He stepped forward and kissed her affectionately on the side of her mouth, a gesture she accepted easily while not taking her eyes off me for a second.

'I didn't think I was ever going to meet any of Mike's family,' she said with a wink that made me like her from the start. She held out her hand and I took it without a thought for my ribs. I was drifting into a daze: the pain-killers maybe, because it was about thirty minutes since I'd popped one at the hospital. I can't remember saying a word, not 'hello', or 'how are you', or 'pleased to meet you'. Once our hands dropped back to our sides I was left staring rather bluntly at the swelling bulge pointed right at me.

Michael caught me doing it and laughed out loud. 'That's not a watermelon stuffed in there, Josh.'

'*Feels* like a watermelon,' said Kelly. 'Be out in a few weeks and I tell you, I'll be glad when I don't have to carry it around in front of me any more.'

'Your mother reckons babies are more trouble outside than in,' said Michael, enjoying himself openly as he teased her with things they must have talked about between themselves.

Kelly made a disgruntled harumphing noise behind her nose. 'Yeah, well it's twenty years since she had any first-hand experience and if you ask me, she's forgotten. Come on in, Josh. Have you had any breakfast?'

As she turned away towards the door the long flowing skirt of her dress twirled with her then danced a jig around her legs as she entered the house. I followed as though I had been commanded by a genie, and the offer of breakfast wasn't a bad inducement either.

The house was pretty basic, a living room first up, with furniture that didn't match and a television perched on two plastic milk crates turned upside-down. It wasn't very tidy, but who was I to say so? Josh Tambling, the guy who carpeted his bedroom with dirty clothes and CDs and half-a-dozen books all open and upside-down beside his bed.

Kelly led me into the kitchen and held out a chair so that I could sit at the laminex table. I was really struggling to keep hold of my thoughts now and it wasn't just the pain-killers. This was all so different from how I had imagined it would be. I was coming to rescue Michael. I had even seen myself getting him to a doctor if he was doing drugs or not taking care of himself. Well, I had ended up at the hospital, all right, but it was Michael who had taken me, in a frigging Holden!

And look at Michael! He was doing well for himself, got a place to live, a job, he's the boss's pin-up boy, and what about Kelly! What about that baby!

I was staring at the bump again. 'Hey, am I going to have a niece or a nephew?'

'We don't know. Asked the doc not to tell us,' Kelly explained, resting her hand on the great shelf sticking out in front of her.

Across the table from me, Michael leaned forward, putting on a serious voice. 'If it's a boy, you'll be an uncle, but you better start praying, Josh, because if it's a girl, that'll make you an aunt,' and he threw himself back into his chair, chuckling away at his own joke. I was so dopey by this time that I had to think about what he had said to see the funny side of it.

Somehow in all of this Kelly had started to make bacon and eggs and slotted some bread into the toaster. I hoed into the toast as soon as it was ready and used the second round, or maybe it was the third, to mop up the runny yolk from two absolutely delicious eggs.

Details are pretty hazy after that. Between them, Michael and Kelly got me into a makeshift bed made of cushions from the old sofa and spare pillows from their own bedroom. After that, I drifted into weird dreams, as though the last two hours hadn't created an incredible fantasy of their own.

chapter twenty

I woke with no idea where I was and sat up suddenly. Bad idea. The pain-killers had worn off, well and truly, and the agony took my breath away. My groan brought Kelly from the kitchen.

'Are you all right, Josh?' she called through the door.

'Yeah, I'm okay. You can come in,' I replied and when she did I asked, 'Do you think Michael could bring me another one of those tablets?'

'I'll get it for you. Mike's working, won't be back until tomorrow morning.'

I looked at my watch and discovered that I had slept for the best part of twenty-four hours. My stomach was empty again, but Kelly quickly fixed that.

'Go have a shower,' she said afterwards. 'I'll get some of Mike's clothes for you to wear.'

Kelly laughed when I came out of the bedroom wearing my brother's clothes. The shirt flapped loosely at my torso like a tent rippling in the breeze and the shorts were in danger of slipping off my hips. 'Tell you what, I'll take you up to town and you can get something that fits a bit better,' she said, stifling another giggle.

'Well . . . actually, I don't have any money. Everything but the bus ticket was in my wallet,' I had to explain, hating the self-pity that crept into my voice.

'Oh, you don't need to worry. Mike and I will pay.'

So she got behind the wheel of the Commodore, her baby bump leaving barely enough room to steer and took me to a shopping centre that didn't look any different from Westfield in Hurstville. I picked out a new pair of shorts, jocks and a couple of cheap T-shirts while Kelly looked at baby clothes.

'I'll bet you're hungry again already,' she said when it was all done. 'Time for some chips,' and she immediately made a beeline for the KFC counter. She wanted the chips more than I did and the way she'd used me as an excuse made her seem so natural, so human. It wasn't hard to see why Michael liked her.

'Why doesn't Mike have much to do with his family?' she asked when we were sitting among the mushroom field of tables all bolted to the floor in the food court. 'Can you tell me, Josh? I thought at first that he had come up the hard way, you know, with no parents to speak of and no money. But then I'd hear him brag to our friends that his dad sells new cars down in Sydney, a real hot-shot salesman. Is it true?'

'Yeah, Dad sells Holdens. He's pretty good at it.'

'There, I didn't think he was lying. He gets on fine with my mum, you know. They tease each other something dreadful. He says she should be ashamed of having a daughter up the duff at only twenty and she says what's wrong with that? She had me at nineteen. Always laughing, scoring points off each other. I can't work it out, what he's got against his own mum and dad.'

She stopped talking, waiting for me to explain.

Why doesn't my brother have anything to do with us? The reasons seemed obvious enough when I left Sydney. Back then I carried an image of Michael in my head, of an angry guy with a restless heart running away from a world that had become too hard for him. The further he ran from us, the more unhappy he would have become – that's the way I saw it, and I'd hoped to bring him home, all the way back into our family where he could be happy again, for our sakes, as much as his.

But none of this would have made any sense to Kelly because it didn't have anything to do with the Michael she knew. I shook my head. 'He's different from what he was like at home, in the last few years before he left, anyway. How did *you* meet him?'

'In a hotel,' she replied, eager to share the story with me. 'I was serving drinks one Friday night when he came in with a trawler crew. We got talking and I gave him my phone number. Went from there, I suppose. He wasn't like the other guys I've been out with. There's a kind of energy in him, don't you think? Takes my breath away, sometimes.'

She sucked on the straw of the milkshake she'd bought to wash down the chips, and stared over my shoulder as though she was hoping to spot Michael in the crowd. 'He was so unreal about the baby, you know. It was an accident, getting pregnant, I mean,' and a wink locked me into their secret. 'I was a bit afraid about telling him, actually, but afterwards we just stood there looking at each other and we knew without saying a word that we both wanted it.'

She put her hand on her swollen stomach and said, 'This and your brother were the things I needed to get my bum into gear. I was just drifting before he came along. He's so good to me.' Her straw made gurgling, farting sounds at the bottom of the milkshake, the noises Mum always stopped us from making.

'What about you, Josh? Are you in love with someone? Have you got a girlfriend?'

'Yeah. Two separate people, though.' The words just slipped out, simple and shocking. 'No, no, it's not true,' I insisted, but the words had scurried away like cockroaches.

Kelly stared at me, ignoring my denial. 'You sly old dog. I'll have to watch you Tambling men. Come on,' she said, starting to slowly and awkwardly leave her chair. 'I'll show you all the beautiful sights of Mackay. Should take at least ten minutes,' and she laughed at her own joke just as Michael would have done.

I spent the rest of the day with Kelly, except for a couple of hours in the afternoon when she took a nap on the breezy back verandah. Carrying around a great melon like that must tire you out. Then it was dinner and TV and an early retreat to my make-shift bed.

*

I woke on Thursday morning to hear Michael's voice drifting in from the kitchen, but he was shattered after working thirty-six hours straight out there on the ocean so once we had finished eating around the laminex table, he went to bed and didn't surface until mid-afternoon.

Wide awake then and with all the small talk of a first meeting used up, he didn't know quite what to say to me. 'Would you like to take a closer look at the *Jeannie Mills*?' he asked finally.

'The what!'

'The trawler I work on. Trevor Mills' boat.'

'Oh . . . yeah, sure.' I didn't know what to say to my brother, either. I might have found him after all but the rest of my vague plans had long since gone the way of my wallet, my iPod and my bag.

Kelly came with us to escape the heat of the house because Mackay hadn't become any cooler since I nearly melted into the pavement on that first morning.

'Gets like this sometimes,' said Michael. 'Feels like it's building up to a storm later in the week. I'll put the airconditioning on for you,' and with a laugh, he rolled down his window. Kelly and I did the same but even the fluttering wind didn't cool my skin so much as suck every drop of the moisture from my body. At least the breeze at the marina carried a little of the ocean's cool.

'Careful, careful,' Michael fussed as we helped Kelly across the gap between the jetty and the trawler's hull. I climbed gingerly after her and managed to avoid jarring my ribs.

The sharp taste of the sea crept up my nose and invaded my mouth, a mixture of salt, the stink that even fresh fish gives off and a faint whisper of the ocean's foamy freshness. Heavy nets, gathered in neat folds, formed a canopy above us that blocked the sun's intensity and left the deck surprisingly dark. In fact, there was quite a jumble of ropes and pulleys and enormous lights up there, much of it hanging from a pair of long booms sitting upright against the sides of the trawler like folded pterodactyl's wings.

While I inspected this impressive array, Michael began a rapid-fire monologue. 'She was refitted only six years ago. Four blade prop and a Fiat engine, V8 no less, twin disc gearbox.'

'He's not here to buy the damned thing, Mike,' Kelly interrupted.

My brother looked a little crestfallen but quickly recovered when I asked, 'Can I see inside the cabin?'

'The wheelhouse, Josh, the wheelhouse. No, sorry, Trev keeps the keys, but you can take a look through here.' He led me to the window. 'The depth sounder is state-of-the-art. Has to be in these waters, the way the ocean floor fluctuates.'

He went on about booms and winches and net capacities. 'Winching in the net's the tricky part. Got to watch the tension on the cables. Guys have been killed by snapped cables. They whip back, cut you in half if you're not careful.'

'Shit! Are you serious?' This didn't come from me. Kelly had gone white under her tropical tan.

Michael saw his mistake too late. 'It's all right, don't worry.

Never happens now. Trev's got tension limiters on all the winches.'

Kelly wasn't so sure. 'I don't want this baby to end up an orphan.'

'He'd still have you.'

'He's going to have a father, too. Not like me.'

'He will, he will,' and to allay her fears even further, he said, 'I was just bullshitting to Josh, here. Got to show off to my own brother while I've got the chance.'

'It looks like hard work to me. And those cuts,' I said, pointing at the graffiti of scabs and scars on his hands.

'Yeah, it's hard,' he replied vaguely, as though he had never thought about it before.

'Do you get seasick, Mike?'

'Did at first. Left a trail of chunder right through the Whitsundays. It's funny because that was the first question they asked me at Centrelink and I told them, no, I'd be fine.'

'So you've been here all the time, ever since you left us in Sydney.'

'Christ, no. A bit over a year, that's all.'

'You never told me where you were. Mum always asked, every time you called and I could never tell her.'

As I spoke, I saw that Kelly was watching him, too, waiting for his answers as much as I was.

'I called from all over, Josh. Don't remember half the places. You know I went up to Surfers, first, with Ricky and Nathan and Nathan's girlfriend.'

I didn't recognise the names but I remembered Mum and Dad had said he'd gone to Surfers.

'We had a falling-out, you might say, and I went to Brisbane for a couple of weeks with this other guy. By the time I came back to the coast, Ricky and the rest'd gone home to Sydney. Bugger them, I thought and I started hitching north.'

'On your own.'

'No law against it.'

'But you had no money.'

'Yeah, tell me about it,' he grinned, trying to make a joke out of it and watching Kelly closely. 'I slept under bridges, ate with the down-and-outs when the do-gooder van came around, did some fruit picking around Emerald. That was hard. It was so bloody hot, but we had some good laughs back at the hostel. Those backpackers know how to have a good time.'

'I saw some here in Mackay,' I answered drily, though neither Michael nor Kelly seemed to notice.

'Mostly I just kept moving and the further away from Sydney, the stronger I felt, sort of free.'

'Why'd you stop, then?' asked Kelly.

''Cause I got fed up with being broke.'

'Tell me about it,' I said, echoing his earlier words. 'I was broke for two days and it nearly killed me.'

'Yeah, well, we've got something in common then, eh? Mackay looked as good a place as any so I went into Centrelink and they asked me if I got seasick.' He brightened up now that the story had returned to familiar territory.

'Then you met Kelly in the pub,' I said, connecting up the dots.

'You know about that, do you?' His eyes left me and fell on Kelly where they much preferred to be. 'Just as well I had some money in my pocket by then, or I could never have swept you off your feet.'

'Too right, I don't come cheap.'

'Meeting Kelly, well, I was ready for something new.'

'You certainly started something new in here,' Kelly teased good-naturedly as she patted her bulge.

No one spoke for a few seconds, until Kelly said, 'Come on, you two. If you're going to tell stories, tell me the ones I haven't heard yet, about this mysterious family you both spring from. All I know so far is that you grew up in the big smoke and your dad sells cars.'

'Holdens,' we both said together then stared at each other until Kelly leaned forward and with a wicked gleam in her eye whispered, 'You two aren't identical twins, or anything, are you?'

'Identical! Josh and me? Jesus, Kel, Josh doesn't even drop lolly papers on the footpath.'

'Bullshit!'

Kelly cut across us impatiently. 'You're avoiding the question, the pair of you.'

'You mean he hasn't told you the rest of it, about Dad, about who he is?'

Kelly shook her head. 'Just the cars . . . the Holdens,' she corrected herself. 'Come on, out with it. What's so special about this father of yours?'

Why not? I turned to her, about to explain, when Mike stopped me. 'No, tell her about Mum.' It was an order, put bluntly and backed up with a serious glare.

'Mum, oh, she's shorter than you, Kelly, . . . she's got dark hair, um, works part-time. How old would she be, Michael? Past fifty, anyway. You'll like her, I'm sure. Pretty quiet.'

'Pretty quiet!' my brother interrupted. 'Josh, you're making Mum sound like the most boring woman alive. Mum's not quiet. She always had the radio on in the house when I was a kid. Not surprising since she used to be on the radio years ago, you know, on the air, a personality. That's it, you make her sound like she's got no personality. She's . . . what's the word . . . vivacious, that's it, Mum's bloody vivacious when she gets going.'

He saw me lost for words and kept going. 'She used to dance sometimes, if she liked the song they were playing on the radio, and she didn't mind who saw her.'

News to me, but I didn't argue.

'All right, so your mother's a vivacious radio personality,' said Kelly, exaggerating deliberately. 'What about your father?'

Michael left it to me, though after his performance about Mum, I felt sheepish telling the story. 'He was a famous League player, one of the best.'

'You mean top-level stuff, like the Broncos.'

'The Broncos,' I sniffed automatically. 'Dad played for St George. Graeme Langlands was his team-mate, he played against Bob Fulton and Arthur Beetson.' I managed to stop myself before the word legend got an airing. Just as well, too, because Michael had crossed his arms and was looking down at his feet as though he couldn't wait for the story to finish.

But it wasn't going to finish in a hurry, not with Kelly picking up the excitement. 'I don't believe this. Mum and I have been fans for years. All those matches the three of us watched on the tele last winter and you didn't say a word. Your father was that good, eh? What about you, Mike, did you play?'

A lazy breeze sniffed at the nets above our heads, making the pulleys and the ropes sway and the entire boat creak, deep in its timbers. Mike looked up, arms still folded protectively across his stomach and sighed as though he had been waiting for this question. 'Yeah, I played a bit as a kid.'

'He was good, too,' I added, to set things straight. 'Could have been in the Firsts at Fidelis if he hadn't given it away.'

If the look Mike sent me had been a punch, I would've been laid out cold on the deck right now. But it was too late.

'Why'd you give it away, then?' Kelly asked Michael innocently.

'I just did, okay,' he shouted, and for the first time since I'd arrived in Mackay, the Michael of my memories revealed himself.

And just as quickly, that person was gone. He strode across the deck to put his arm around Kelly's shoulder and kiss her above the ear. 'I'm sorry, I'm sorry,' he whispered, followed by words too soft for me to hear.

Kelly had stiffened in surprise when Michael snapped at her so sharply but his immediate contrition and the tenderness of his touch made her relax just as quickly. Still, the tiny eruption left a silence in the angular confines of the trawler. I wasn't saying a thing, was I. If there had been only my brother and me among the hanging nets and the salty stink of fish, the topic would have died there. Not this time, though. This was something I was starting to learn about my brother, the presence of Kelly in everything he said and did. He stepped away from her and went back to leaning against the hull. The silence lingered, Kelly's silence, carried in her eyes as she watched him and waited patiently.

'It was because of that bloody Terry Vickers,' said Mike, savagely.

The name hung in the air, as heavy as the nets above us. 'Who's he?' Kelly asked.

Nothing from Michael; it was up to me, then. 'A coach with St George, a talent scout. Terry was kind of Dad's mentor, the one who signed him up for the club when he was younger than me. They're still friends.'

Kelly nodded but it didn't help her understand. Her eyes went back to Mike and so did mine because I didn't understand yet, either.

'What was wrong with Terry Vickers?' I prompted him.

'Silly old bugger.' He unfolded his arms and pushed off the hull, standing straight and tanned and looking up towards the tip of the enormous boom above my head. This was his place, where he was in charge, where he was the successful one. 'Terry didn't just go on about how good Dad was in his heyday. He had to tell anyone who'd listen that he'd seen Phil

Tambling as a teenager, what a talent he was, even then, and how you and me, Josh, we weren't a patch on our old man, no matter how hard we tried, we'd never be as good. "Wasting our time strapping on a boot," that's what he said. Those very words. I wanted to punch his lights out, the frigging loud-mouth. Wish I had.'

That was it? He'd stopped playing football because of some stupid remark. Terry Vickers was a clown, we all knew that. Even Dad told him to stick a sock in it now and then.

'It was more than that, wasn't it, Mike,' said Kelly gently.

The breath worked in and out of my brother's lungs. He was back staring at the deck again, restless and vulnerable and maybe wishing I had never turned up at this marina. 'It wasn't the football. The footy wasn't important. The rest of it is too hard to explain. It was like having a Terry Vickers everywhere I looked reminding me who my father was, everywhere I went, everything I did. "You're Phil Tambling's son, aren't you?" I can't explain, Kel,' he pleaded. 'Look, I don't want to talk about it, not here, not on the boat.' Mike swept an arm towards me. 'Josh has come up to Mackay to visit me. All that stuff was back in Sydney. Come on,' he added, striding purposefully to the opposite side of the trawler where he waited with out-stretched arms to help Kelly up onto the jetty. 'Let's go to the beach.'

nstead of turning west towards the centre of Mackay, Mike pointed the Commodore north and after a few minutes turned down a track that ran behind some low dunes.

The beach was ours. 'Everyone's gone home for dinner,' he said, glancing at his watch. 'You don't see a lot of people, anyway. Can't swim at this time of the year 'cause of the stingers. We often come down here for a walk when it's too hot in the house, don't we Kel?'

The day was wilting towards sunset as though the languid tropical heat sapped its energy as much as ours. We began to walk slowly northwards along the high-water mark of the darting waves. The breeze was stronger here and the water invigorating around our ankles. The waves curling just a few metres off-shore weren't much to speak of but they added a rhythmic shush and sigh as backdrop to our voices. My brother's momentary anger had been left behind at the marina.

Kelly walked between us, holding Mike's hand. The further

we went, the more she waddled like a duck in the uncertain footing of the sand.

'Are you okay?' Mike asked when he noticed.

'Yeah, don't worry about me. I'll be glad when I can carry the baby in my arms, though.'

'When's it due? You haven't told me the date.'

'Twentieth of Feb,' Mike answered, looking ahead along the beach. 'You wouldn't believe it, Josh, that's exactly a year after we met. What do you reckon, Kel, can we bring the little one down here once he's arrived? Get some salt air into his lungs.'

'Could be *her* lungs,' Kelly corrected him.

'Yeah, yeah,' laughed Mike. 'Be out-numbered then, won't I. Two sheilas and one bloke.' It didn't sound like he minded the idea, though. Seagulls squabbled over the right to scurry, stiff-legged, behind us in case we spilled largesse as we walked. Mike watched them peck and posture then said brightly, 'Hey, Josh, do you remember walking along the beach like this with Mum and Dad? There was one time Hayley got tired of walking so Dad put her on his shoulders.'

'Yeah, I remember, but Hayley doesn't. It was on the Gold Coast, wasn't it? Christmas time . . .'

'No, it wasn't Christmas, Josh. It was cold on the beach that day. Mum was wearing Dad's windcheater, it flapped around in the wind. I know, it was September holidays and it wasn't the Gold Coast, it was the beach at Forster.'

He stopped, making Kelly and me do the same. 'Mum didn't want that day to end, you know. She said she wished the sun would stop where it was so we could keep walking forever.' His words faltered and while he stared straight ahead, it wasn't this beach he was seeing. 'You know what I did, I climbed the dunes and held up my hands, so that it looked like I was stopping the sun from sinking any lower.'

He turned round quickly, looking at the sun. 'I'll show you,' he cried. Backing twenty or thirty metres up the beach, he raised his arms.

I could see how he did it so perfectly now, but as a ten-year-old it had seemed like magic. He used the shadows cast by his own elongated body, moving along the beach a little way until he was in position then adjusting his arms until the silhouette of his cupped palms touched Kelly's face. Beside her I saw the too-bright ball burning my brother's hands.

Kelly stood, fascinated, shielding her eyes as best she could and laughing. 'How did you work it out?'

'Oh, I don't know,' Mike called as he jogged to join us again at the water's edge. 'Just came to me, something I could do for Mum, to make her laugh. She was always calling me her special boy.'

'You're still her special one,' I told him.

His eyes flicked back to me and the easy smile died instantly on his lips. After a second or two, he looked away again, out to sea this time, and said nothing.

With Kelly taking each step a little slower than the last, we returned to the Commodore and went home for dinner.

chapter twenty-two

Michael didn't have to work again until Saturday night. He took Kelly for an appointment with her obstetrician on Friday morning, leaving me in the oven of their house as the temperature nudged into the mid-thirties. I'd quickly learned that the coolest place, if anywhere in Mackay could be called cool, was on their back verandah. When they returned, I was half-asleep in Kelly's hammock.

'Everything's fine,' Michael announced with a broad grin. 'Next time we see the doc will be in the labour ward, he reckons.'

'Only a man could sound pleased about that,' Kelly complained, pushing him playfully on the shoulder. 'Blokes don't have to do any of the labouring.'

I vacated the hammock where she immediately replaced me. Mike brought us each a glass of cold water from the fridge and then sat in a tattered, overstuffed armchair Kelly's mother had given them because she didn't want it at her place any more. He could have been a king on his throne, if you ignored the Stubbies and thongs. I rested my bum on the railing with my back against the wall, feeling right at home.

'Josh, about your wallet.'

'I'm never going to get it back now.' I pulled at my new shirt and shorts, saying, 'I can't pay you back for these duds until I'm home again in Sydney.'

'You don't have to pay us back. They're a late Christmas present, okay. But did you have any cards in your wallet?'

'Like credit cards, you mean? No, just my key card.'

'Yeah, thought so,' he sighed, glancing at Kelly in the private way that couples have. I'd seen Mum and Dad do the same thing. 'We'd better cancel it. Anything else in your wallet we need to worry about?'

'No, just my learner's permit.'

'Learner's permit!' my brother repeated, suddenly wide-eyed and disbelieving. 'Hey, you're seventeen. Of course you're learning.' He was excited now and stood up suddenly. 'So how good are you, then? Driving in traffic yet?'

'Yeah,' I replied proudly. 'But only in the side streets around home. Been learning in Mum's Astra.'

'Oh, what!' he snarled in mock horror. 'Bloody sheila's car if ever there was one. On your feet,' he commanded. 'Time you drove a real car.'

He meant the Commodore, of course. After the Astra, the sheer size of it intimidated me, not to mention the noise when I pressed the accelerator and the power I could feel under my foot. Michael ignored my nervousness. 'Come on, drop the clutch and let's see what you can do.'

It was a wild ride. Nearly put us into a palm tree at the first corner. That wiped the smile off his face and he was soon talking me through everything like Dad. 'Take it easy, change to second, careful on the clutch, that's it . . .'

He made sure we avoided the central part of Mackay and after crossing a long bridge he pointed to a flat stretch of land about the size of a football field coming up on our left. 'Pull off there, Josh. I'll teach you how to stop, the Tambling brothers' way.'

This meant accelerating for about sixty metres and then hitting the brakes hard so that the wheels locked up, making the car slide over the gravel. 'Best to get a feel for it in a place like this. Controlled conditions, eh? No use panicking first time the wheels slide around under you in a bit of dirt.'

It was hair-raising, breath-taking stuff, but it was a fantastic buzz too, something Dad would never let me do in the Astra; not in a million years. After five runs I had to wimp out because my ribs were hurting too much from the impact of the seatbelt. We swapped places for the drive home, but instead of heading off, Mike cut the engine.

'What do you think of Kelly, eh?' he asked, looking across at me from the driver's seat. 'Isn't she great?'

'She's the most beautiful thing I've ever seen.'

Should have seen the look on Michael's face. You'd think he'd won lotto and the Melbourne Cup all on the same day. The words came out like that because I wanted to please him, but they stunned me as well. To be honest, Kelly wasn't really a match for the glamorous models and actors you see on television. Her kind of beauty would be hidden next to a perfect face and elegant gestures. She was happy with her life, with the people she loved and especially the man who loved her, but I couldn't explain any of this to Michael without sounding like a girl.

'Oh, mate, you're right about that,' he assured me eagerly. 'I'm looking forward to this baby. Not going to be easy with me away on the trawler for two or three days sometimes, but Kel's mother lives in West Mackay, so that will take a lot of the pressure off.'

Pressure, mothers. Those words were like triggers in my head. 'Mike, look, the reason I came up here –'.

'You were going to talk me into going home, weren't you, Josh,' he cut in quickly, but without anger or accusation in his voice.

'Yeah, I suppose that was in the back of my mind.'

'I can't go home, Josh. Not yet.'

'I know, I know, but there's stuff you should know, Mike. Mum's cracking up. It's getting real touchy between her and Dad. She blames him for you staying away like this.'

'She's bloody right, too.'

'But she didn't do it. She didn't want you to go. It's not fair that you won't speak to *her*, at least. Dad's the one you're angry with.'

'Of course I am. He threw me out of the house, didn't he? And Mum didn't stop him. Why wouldn't I be angry?'

A silence lingered between us while I built up the courage to say what I had to say, but there was no getting round it, even if it made my brother more angry than he seemed. 'Mike, Dad's absolutely straight in everything he does. He . . .' The next words should have been, *loves you,* but we were two guys sitting in a Commodore in the middle of the skid marks we'd gouged into the gravel. It wouldn't sound right, so I fudged it. 'He cares about you, Mike. He cares about you more than I do, or Hayley, or even Mum.'

Staring ahead through the windscreen, looking at things I couldn't see, he'd heard what I'd really meant to say. The silence hung on uncomfortably until I filled it with the only thing I knew to be true any more. 'Dad's a good man.'

'Oh yeah, I know all about what a good man Phil Tambling is,' Michael raged. 'I heard all the stories about him before you did, Josh, about the struggle he had with his old man, the drunken fart who used to beat them all up every night and twice on Sundays. I know how he faced up to his father, how he knocked him out for the count like some boxer. Well that's his story, Josh. Up here, I'm making my own.'

Michael was silent for almost a minute then continued more calmly, 'We're not carbon copies of Dad, Josh. Sooner or later you have to make your own life. Dad did me a favour, you know, kicking me out like that. Looking at it now, I'm glad he did.' Then he reached across and did that thing with my hair again. 'Made me grow up, you know, become my own man. I can see that. I mean, shit, if he hadn't thrown me out, I would never have met Kelly. Do you know what I'm getting at, Josh? The best things in life are the ones you go out and grab for yourself. That's being your own man.'

I was having trouble keeping my mouth from hanging open while he said this. The woolly-headed bugger was ruining his own argument. Not that it mattered. Mike dropped his voice and took hold of my upper arm, carefully so that he didn't disturb my ribs. 'You'll have to do the same one day, little brother. No matter what a good bloke Dad is, you'll have to break away from him in the end.'

'I don't know. I can't see myself shooting through. Two days living like you did was enough for me.' I didn't say the rest – that really, I was no rebel, that the last thing I wanted was to cause Mum and Dad the grief that Michael had given them these past two years.

He must have guessed what I was thinking, because he smiled, his face looking even more grown-up than when I arrived, and said, 'Not for you, eh? Yeah, well I can understand that, but you'll do it all the same, in your own way, 'cause you're different from Dad, same as I am. Don't be afraid of that, Josh.' As he reached for the ignition, he added softly, 'Like I was.'

chapter twenty-three

On Saturday morning, I had to say something about going back to Sydney. It was a day and a half's ride in the bus and I was expected home by Monday afternoon. The problem, of course, was money. Having come to Mackay to rescue Michael, I was once again completely dependent on him instead.

'Not a problem,' he said with a wink, 'but I'd better ask the accountant, all the same,' he added, to stir Kelly who was moving through the living room like a ghostly blimp at that moment. 'Can we afford to pay for Josh's bus ticket?'

'I'll pay you back,' I assured them instantly.

'You don't need to, Josh,' Kelly responded just as quickly, as she came to stand behind the sofa where Michael was lounging. 'He's making good money on Trev's boat just at the moment.'

Mike put one hand behind his head, the other searching for Kelly's until she took hold of it, and you should have seen the pleasure on his face at what she'd said.

'I've got plenty in the bank, too, though. I worked right through the holidays.'

'Then you should have the fun of spending it,' said Mike, who still wouldn't take me seriously.

'But I want to send you the money. It means a lot to me.' Perhaps I overdid the insistence in my voice. It was enough to make Mike turn right round and exchange a bemused glance with Kelly.

'Okay, okay, keep your shirt on, little brother,' he said when he was facing me again. 'I'll have to stop calling you that if you're going to push me around.'

I knew what bus Dave was taking back to Sydney from Port Macquarie and after a bit of explaining on the phone to the booking agent, I got myself a seat on the same one. All I needed then was a bus back to Brisbane. Easy. Mike paid for it all by credit card.

'My bus comes through here at half-past one in the morning, though,' I had to tell them when it was all booked.

'I'll be out to sea by then,' Mike said with a disappointed frown. 'Kel will have to take you into MacAlister Street.'

The final day in Mackay hung low and lazy around us like the tropical storm that was slowly, finally building towards an afternoon downpour. It was taking its time, teasing, pumping up the humidity to stifling heights as we sat down to an early tea before Mike headed out on the trawler. The meal started quietly with the unspoken knowledge in each of us that I would be gone by the time he came back and we hadn't yet talked about when we would see each other again.

Then, into this still and silent pool Kelly lobbed a stone. 'Josh, I've told Mike he should go with you, tonight, back to Sydney to see your parents.' Then she reached across and squeezed his hand, adding with a teasing smile, 'But you're a stubborn bugger; I've learned that much about you, haven't I?'

My brother's face remained solemn and his lips silent, leaving Kelly to explain the things he wouldn't say. 'It's the baby, you see. It could come any time, really, and then there's his job, of course.'

'I can't leave Trev in the lurch,' said Mike, breaking his silence at last. 'Not at this time of the year when he needs every hand he's got to keep the boat working. I'm sorry, Josh, I can't make any promises about coming home.'

'You are home.' The words came out as one of those easy repetitions that can sound so clever, yet I had never said anything more honestly in my whole life. Maybe I had to hear myself say it before I knew it was true, a truth that simply popped out, unexpected and irretrievable. 'You don't belong in Sydney, any more. You live here with Kelly. You can't just up and leave. The brother I knew back in Sydney might have done that.'

I don't know what made me say those last words. I was on dangerous ground and couldn't find a way off it. 'You've never met that Michael,' I said to Kelly, trying to retrieve the situation, 'same as my mum and dad wouldn't recognise the guy who lives here with you.'

My brother's eyes flared and before I could say any more, he was on his feet and gone from the kitchen.

'Shit, shit, shit! What did I say that for?' I seethed at myself. I'd blown everything now, insulted my brother, hurt him when I had no right to.

'No, Josh, you're wrong about that. They're the same person,' said Kelly. Her response came so calmly and with such disarming conviction that whatever else I'd been going to say died in my throat, leaving a single thought to escape unconsciously.

'I just wish they knew that back in *my* home.'

Yes, *my* home. 'They're hurting, Kelly,' I pleaded, fighting tears now. 'I can't make him understand what it's doing to them. I've tried to tell him, but he's still so angry.'

'No, I don't think he is angry, Josh. Like I said, he's stubborn.'

I kept going, I needed someone to understand. 'It's Mum. She's not as strong as Dad is, not when it comes to this, and he can't see it. If Mike would just talk to them when he rings. He doesn't have to say where he is, just let them hear his voice and maybe they will understand that he's really okay, that there is more to him than they realise, and they don't have to worry. If he'd just let Mum tell him that she loves him.'

Better shut up now. I was lucky, really, that they hadn't thrown me out of their house.

Kelly went after Mike, and finding myself alone in the kitchen, I started on the washing-up. The drone of serious, measured voices seeped through the wall from their bedroom, emphasising my exclusion.

The sun disappeared, the kitchen became unnaturally dark. With the air so laden with moisture, perspiration beaded on my forehead faster than I could wipe it away with my soapy hands. Then there was a flash and seconds later, thunder, distant and bombastic, more a warning than a threat. The palm fronds outside the kitchen window, soldier-still for days, began to move and finally the storm broke over us, quickly overpowering the faint bedroom voices with a thousand tiny hammer strikes on the corrugated iron. What a deluge! It had taken all week to arrive and it wasn't going to disappoint.

With the last of the saucepans draining beside the sink, I went out onto the back verandah to watch the torrential rain cascade from the roof. The air temperature had dropped rapidly outside, bringing a welcome freshness. I cupped my hands in the largest of the waterfalls and enjoyed the vitality of the rain as it splashed onto my wrists. My ribs still ached a little at the effort, reminding me that the journey home wasn't going to be any picnic, but this was a soothing way to say goodbye to the house, to this stamp-sized verandah where I'd watched the two of them together, and talked so easily.

'Josh,' Kelly called from the doorway. I turned to see her beckoning me inside. 'You probably want to see this.' She led me into the living room where Mike was sitting on the edge of the lounge chair with the phone to his ear.

'It's all right, Mum,' he was saying. 'You don't need to cry.

Everything's fine. I'm doing real good, actually. I've got a job and it pays pretty well, depending on the season.'

'Where am I?' Michael sighed and didn't answer until he had taken a couple of slow breaths. 'I'm in North Queensland, Mum. Can't you hear the rain? It's pouring here, right now. Where? Well, I don't want to tell you exactly where yet. Dad? He's there, is he? Look, no, I don't think I want to speak to him, Mum. Just you, okay?'

He sensed my presence behind him and turned towards me, at the same time adding to his last words, '. . . since Josh seems to be on holiday somewhere. Oh, Mum, you don't have to cry. I've got to go now, but I'll ring again to talk to you another time, okay? Bye . . . good . . . Goodbye now.'

Mike stabbed lightly at a button of the cordless phone and sat for a moment staring at his hands. I could just see my mother putting down the phone at the other end of the line and then she would look for Dad, wanting him to hold her, crying, too, maybe, crying tears of joy. At least, that's what I wanted to believe.

And if Mum was elated then Dad would be, too. This was why I had come north and I couldn't help listening to a tiny voice in my head saying, 'You did this, Josh Tambling. You might have cocked things up big time, but you got here and you said what had to be said.'

How good did that feel, those few moments in Mike's lounge room? He looked up at me as he weighed the phone in his hands and something passed between us, as brothers. To describe it would take a whole book, or a song, but I wasn't interested in describing anything. It was great just to feel it.

'It's twenty to seven,' he said, glancing at his watch. 'Better get moving.'

The rain stopped with much less conviction than it began and the sun made a late appearance, hanging diamonds and pearls from every leaf. Mike drove the Commodore to the wharf and left the driver's door open for Kelly who would take the wheel for the return journey.

She kissed Mike and then stepped back for me to say whatever I wanted to say. It came out as thanks, mostly, thanks for looking after me when I arrived here such a wreck, thanks for letting me drive his car.

The wharf was teeming with passengers recently returned from a day-cruise out to the reef, and Michael's eyes roamed anywhere rather than look at me. 'Listen, Josh,' he said finally. 'Tell Dad I don't hate him any more. Tell him . . . tell him, I never did.'

'I can't, Mike. If I tell him anything, he'll know I've been up here to see you. Besides, it won't mean anything until you tell him yourself.'

He thought about this then nodded. 'Yeah, all right. This trip of yours has to be our little secret. As for the rest, well, I'm not making any promises.'

His hand made it all the way to my hair before he changed his mind and let it drop, offering his weathered palm to me, thumb upwards, fingers extended. I shook my brother's hand, muttering a feeble goodbye.

*

At one o'clock, Kelly drove me in to meet the bus and I had to go through my second departure scene in a matter of hours. This time there were waves and even a kiss on the cheek. Women do farewells so much better than guys. I've never hugged a pregnant woman before; it's an awkward sort of manoeuvre and intimate in a way that embarrassed me as much as it comforted.

I left Mackay just as I had arrived, in the darkness of the early hours – and alone.

chapter twenty-four

Nothing had changed. Though I wasn't quite honest enough to admit it on the journey north, I hadn't come just to find my brother. I had come to take Michael home, to give him back to Mum and Dad like something from Clive's suitcase. That wasn't going to happen and this trip had turned out to be a fantasy, no different from last week with Clive when I had tried to muscle my way into his kindness. All I'd managed to do was get myself robbed, beaten up and humiliated.

A pain-killer helped turn my drowsiness into sleep, but there were only a couple left in the packet and I had another night to get through yet. Come on, bus, I thought impatiently, eat up those kilometres, get me to Sydney, to Oatley, to my own place.

The last glimpse of an orange sun reflected in the windows of Brisbane's skyscrapers as the bus hissed to a halt in the Transit

Centre. I'd had enough adventures in the surrounding streets to last a while so I spent the next two hours eating alone in the Transit Centre's kiosk and enjoying the sensation of *not* being on a bus.

Then, a few minutes before nine, I was on the road again. Brisbane was roughly halfway, so every kilometre now brought me closer to Sydney than I was to Mackay. I didn't care any more if it seemed I was retreating, empty-handed. I just wanted to rest my aching body in my own soft bed.

The pain grew steadily worse. When one tablet didn't make much difference, I popped a second: the last one in fact. I'd pay for that decision tomorrow, most likely, but all I wanted was for sleep to beckon me aboard its painless bus, with my own dreams at the wheel.

And I did dream! Vivid colours burst behind my eyes until they became faces, the usual suspects, the faces that had set up camp in my mind these last few weeks. Mum and Dad were there and Michael, now with Kelly at his side in that floaty white dress. Gemma too and Mr Habden in a coat with A-pluses sown all over it. Weird! And Clive, of course, off to one side where he preferred to be, smiling his round-cheeked smile. They were all laughing, so happy, Mum most of all, as though this was her party. She was talking into a telephone and Mike was answering her, his hand tight within Kelly's.

We were all outside. It was a clear night and I could see every detail of the constellations, more than ever before, right to the edge of the universe.

'Look at the stars,' I called to them, amazed. 'They don't have to mean anything. They're just there.'

They didn't seem to hear me, or else they didn't care. I went closer, determined to make them look, but instead, my eyes were drawn to their faces, picking them out separately and wondering what they meant to me until I sensed an overwhelming goodness in the presence of each one.

They made room for a new face among them. It was my own. How could I be in two places at once? Ah, but this was my own universe where the only rules were the ones I gave meaning to.

Clive was calling to me. 'You found it, then. You found something for my suitcase.'

Did I? But there was no need for an answer. The sound of his gentle voice and the sight of my face beside my father's was filling me with the uninhibited glee I remembered from childhood Christmases around the Tambling family tree, the same sensation that had burned for a fleeting moment in Michael's lounge room. A wave of happiness, a wind, an entire world of unbearable ecstasy hovered within my reach and I wanted to grab hold, to bury myself inside it forever.

The intensity of emotion brought me awake. An afterglow lingered as I slowly rose up from sleep, aware gradually that my head was wedged against something hard and constantly vibrating – a window. There was a woman beside me. I was in a bus hurtling down a highway.

I didn't want the feeling to leave me, but I had no control over it. What was it, how did I get it back? I knew that it could not be now, nor any time I chose, perhaps, but I craved the chance to experience it again.

Through the window, the sky was streaked with a pale light and over the next twenty minutes I watched, fascinated, as the sun came up. The final seconds before it broke free of the earth created an optical illusion, as though the sun was born from a liquid landscape that flopped suddenly back into place once the great orange ball had severed contact.

Egyptians had once worshipped the sun and as it climbed relentlessly above the horizon to become an enormous eye staring with nuclear ferocity, the idea made sense. No wonder those ancient people thought it was a god lording over them, watching their every move.

Not me, though. I lived in the twenty-first century where the sun was no eye at all, saw nothing, judged nothing, made no decisions about who would prosper and who would die. Only human beings do that sort of thing: the strange habit of judging ourselves and feeling something deeply personal because of it.

I wasn't sure what to make of my dream, but judging myself seemed a part of it. In the back of my mind, while I went over and over it, was the face that had been missing – Alicia's – and as the ecstasy of my dream faded, this omission troubled me more and more. With so much else going on, I'd barely given her a thought. My body shuddered involuntarily, remembering what might have happened at Dave's party. And I hadn't even called her.

'You've been a real bastard to her, Tambling,' I whispered.

So, should I break up with her? That would only hurt her

more, wouldn't it? No, I'd be a better boyfriend. That was the right thing to do, the very least I could do.

But if I had been hoping this decision would bring back the ecstasy of my dream, then I was disappointed.

chapter twenty-five

J ust after seven-thirty, the bus pulled into Port Macquarie and there were Dave and Tom Marcovic to meet it. The other passengers weren't too pleased with our boisterous reunion and the black eye didn't help.

'What happened to you?' roared Dave from five rows away.

'A surfing accident,' I said, with a wink. 'Don't you remember?'

'What the hell are you talking about!'

Dave always was a bit slow to catch on. 'My parents are going to hear that a board smashed into my face on our first morning at Port Macquarie, right? And you are going to back me up.'

The light came on in my friend's face, quickly morphing into his familiar smirk but at least the confusion helped to deflect his interest in the real cause.

'Did you find your brother?' Tom asked.

'Yeah,' I said in a measured voice. 'Yeah, I found him.'

'And?' Dave demanded.

I didn't want to talk about it, not in public like this and not with them. Luckily, the guys were blocking other passengers and had to push on down the aisle to their allotted seats. From Newcastle, Dave rang his parents who would ring mine in turn to let them know our arrival time. I told the guys about my missing bag and together we concocted a story to cover for it – stolen off the beach at Port Macquarie on our last day.

Mum's face was among the small crowd waiting for the bus when it pulled up outside Central Station. 'My face?' I said, touching it as though the scab was a surprise to me. The rogue surfboard story worked a treat, though Mum was a bit sceptical about the stolen bag.

'Did you report it to the police?'

'No, but I've cancelled my ATM card.'

She sniffed as though I was taking it all too casually, but she didn't go on about it because she had her own story to tell. 'We've had a breakthough with Michael. He rang on Saturday, asked to speak to me especially. Even told us he's in North Queensland!'

'I'll bet you're pleased!'

'Oh, Josh, you should have been there,' she replied quickly, cramming more relief into a handful of words than seemed possible.

'No word on him coming home?' I asked rather deliberately.

She shook her head. 'It's the first step, though. He still wouldn't speak to Dad, but he sounded happy, Josh.'

So did Mum. She started to fill me in on other things that

had happened. 'Your blazer came back from the uniform shop and there was a letter for you, too. I put in on your desk.'

At home I went straight to my room and just about kissed the back of the door once I'd closed it behind me. The blazer beckoned from where Mum had hung it, on the outside knob of the wardrobe. Couldn't help inspecting the newly embroidered words and because Mum had mentioned the two things together, I expected the letter to be about school as well. It wasn't, though; it had been hand delivered, with just my name written in biro on the envelope.

I ripped it open and began to read:

Dear Josh,

I can't believe you would treat me like this. You don't care about me at all and I'm fed up with it. I didn't really want to go to that party at Dave's in the first place and then you go and stand me up. I waited round for you for hours and you didn't have the courtesy to call me. I ended up going on my own and had to lie the whole time about why you weren't there with me.

Then you go away surfing without even ringing up to apologise. Maybe I could have forgiven you if you had at least done that. I've even waited two days to see whether you would ring up from wherever you went. But still not a word from you and now I am so angry I don't care any more.

I am writing this letter to you because I don't want to have to speak to you again. Our relationship is over. I am dumping you and I wish I had done it weeks ago. (She had scribbled out the next few words but I could still read, *I can't believe that I was going to . . .*)

Don't try to ring me to make it up. I am over you already.
There are plenty of other girls who are going to hear what you
are like, too. I don't know why I wanted to go out with you in
the first place. You never really cared about me. You were always
more interested in your stupid band and when it wasn't music
you were boring my head off with stuff that no one wants to talk
about.

GOODBYE
Alicia.

Oh, shit! It didn't help that every furious word was true.
I went straight out to the kitchen to get the cordless phone,
tapping in the number before I was halfway back to my room.
Seconds after the door clicked shut behind me, Alicia's mother
was on the line.

'It's Josh Tambling. Could I please speak to Alicia?'

The long pause confirmed that my chances were close to
zero. 'I don't know if she's home, Josh,' she said finally. 'I'll just
go and check.'

Alicia was home all right or else her mother wouldn't have
clamped her palm so tightly over the mouthpiece. I didn't hear
a thing for nearly two minutes, then, 'Josh, Alicia's not here,
but she was pretty clear that she doesn't want to talk to you.
She said something about a letter she sent. Maybe you should
read that. In the meantime, it's probably best that you don't
ring here at all.'

If I went round there, they'd set the dogs on me, most

233

likely, but I didn't seriously consider going over to her place. It was finished, like she said, and the awful thing was I was glad. More than that – incredibly relieved.

Alicia had let me off the hook, even if she wouldn't quite see it that way. At the same time, part of me felt cheated. I'd been an absolute mongrel to Alicia and now there was no hope of making things right. I stayed flat on my back for the next few days, read a bit, but just as often the book lay open across my chest while I stared at the ceiling. Were those promises on the bus genuine? Or did they condemn me to a different kind of acting, pretending to care for Alicia to make her happy, instead of pretending so she'd . . . Yeah, well.

Late on Tuesday, Hayley burst into my room. 'Hey, Josh, Mum's taking me down to get some DVDs. You want anything?'

I shook my head but before she charged off up the hall, I asked, 'Hayles, have you ever seen Mum dance?'

'What, with Dad? Are you kidding!'

'No, around the house. Mike said . . .' Oops, just caught myself in time. 'I mean, have you ever seen her jigging around the place with the radio on?'

She still thought I was kidding.

Mike was in my head a lot, and Kelly, of course. I'd fallen a little bit in love with her, not in a romantic sense, but as a person you felt good about, someone you're going to like for the rest of your life. She'd been in my dream and that was another thing that filled my head over those listless days while my ribs slowly knitted together. Those lunar faces stared at me, watched me, but at the same time formed a barrier that wasn't easy to break through, even if I wanted to. They were all people who meant the world to me.

One of them was Gemma and this set me thinking. I might not have given Alicia a thought during my travels, but Gemma had been there, barefooted and waving from a table in the corner of my thoughts, perhaps because she had come to see me at the Lost Property Office on my last day when I was so stirred up. Hey, I was free now. It didn't take long to work out what that meant. By Thursday my ribs were much better; I could breathe without pain and an excursion outside the house was definitely on the cards. I rang the Kominskys', expecting to get Steve, but instead Gemma's voice was right there in my ear.

'Steve will be home about lunch time. Why don't you come over then?'

That was perfect. Mum was working so I had to take the train two stations and then a bus, arriving at the Kominskys' door about eleven, hoping that Steve wouldn't be early. Gemma looked better than I remembered, better than I had ever seen her. Her hair was free of the standard ponytail that morning, spilling out behind her ears and onto her shoulders. The light from the window caught it at an angle, painting one side with a ginger sheen and kissing the tips with dabs of gold, while the rest turned to dark brown by degrees the nearer it lay to her neck.

She shifted some cushions on the sofa so we could sit down, moving easily, without a care for who was watching yet rewarding those who did with the sense of someone who was comfortable with herself and wonderfully free of tricks and pretention. Alone with her, engrossed by her, I wanted to sit and talk for hours, to tell her everything that had happened since we parted at Central Station. Gemma would listen and then tell me honestly what she thought and the weight pressing on me would become lighter.

'I've heard that things aren't so good between you and Alicia,' she said, watching my face cautiously to see how I reacted.

Did I grimace? 'Not so good, no. In fact she dumped me, by letter,' I said with a laugh to cover the embarrassment. 'It was waiting for me when I got back from . . . from Port Macquarie.'

'By letter. That's awful. At least she could have –'

I cut her off before she worked up a steaming head of indignation on my behalf. 'No, she was right to do it that way. I wasn't really interested in her anyway, so it's probably a good thing.'

Gemma didn't say anything to this, not even more words of commiseration, which I half-expected. This surprised me, but her silence and serious expression raised my hopes for what I was going to say next.

'I know this is all kind of sudden, Gemma, when I've just broken up with Alicia, but one of the reasons we broke up was that I'd rather go out with you. Ever since I met you again, in the garage when the guys and I were practising, I've just thought, wow, you're special. I'd really like to be with you.'

I stopped, my rehearsed lines simply petering out. Gemma still hadn't said a word. If I kept rambling on now, I'd sound like an idiot. It was her turn to speak.

Not that I took my eyes off her for a second and this was slowly turning from a pleasure into agony. Words aren't the only way to tell what a person is thinking, or even how they are feeling, especially when emotions can go either way. Even before she spoke, her eyes, the set of her shoulders, her hands, all whispered their clues.

'Oh, Josh, I wish you'd told me this before. You see, I guessed things weren't going well between you and Alicia. It was easy to see, really, to me, anyway, so I knew, probably before you did, that it was going to end. And I do like you and the way we could talk about things like in the front yard that night, Josh, and at the station when I came to see you at work.

'But didn't you understand why I came to see you? I came to ask what you wanted to do, that maybe you wanted to get something going, but you didn't say anything. I tried to tell you – I had to know because of Neven. He was the one who wanted me to come along on New Year's Eve. He made Steve invite me, and a couple of days later he asked me out. I really like him, but I really liked you too, Josh. That's why I came to the Lost Property Office that day, to see if you wanted . . . Oh, Josh, I'm with Neven now and he's a lot of fun. We've been out together just about every day while you guys were up the north coast. I'm sorry, but I can't go out with you.'

I went straight home from Gemma's place and lay down in my room, and for the next couple of days only came out for meals.

What an idiot I'd been. Gemma had actually come to the Lost Property Office to give me a chance to say something, but I'd been too distracted to realise. Over and over I replayed the moment when her mobile rang in the kiosk and she glanced down at Neven's number on the screen. 'Should I answer it, Josh?' If only I'd known what she was really asking.

Neven called to arrange another practice session at Steve's house. I couldn't face it and put him off, telling myself that the guitar was too heavy for my ribs. Might have been the truth, might not. Eventually, my mood around the house was too obvious to ignore. Mum tried to draw me out at the dinner table, but I managed to shrug her off with, 'I'm okay. Just tired.'

That night Dad came to my room. 'You're off the hook now, Josh,' he said in such a repetition of the way I had thought about Alicia that all the guilt flooded back into my bones. He must have seen my pained expression and wondered what he had said to unsettle me. 'You don't have to be piggy-in-the-middle any more,' he explained, 'between Michael and us, that's what I mean. I know how much you hated it.'

I relaxed again as quickly as I had taken fright.

'I brought you this,' he went on, holding up a CD case and, without asking whether I wanted to hear it, he slipped the disc into the deck of my stereo. 'Which number is it?' he muttered to himself. A few clicks of the button and he stood up straight, watching me from behind a half-smile as he waited for the song to start. That smile was hiding something, a touch of nervousness maybe? Which left me wondering why until the music kicked in, no intro, the first words coming with the deep opening chord.

Close my eyes and try to sleep,
Her face won't let me be.

It was the Freddy Riebolt song we'd listened to in the Statesman on Christmas Day, only it wasn't a Freddy Riebolt song at all and this wasn't Freddy singing it. This was the original by old Don Jennings himself.

'So what do you think now?' Dad wanted to know when it was finished. 'Is this version better than the one you played in the car?'

I put Freddy's version in the player and we listened together.

'He didn't change it at all,' Dad noted seriously. 'No need, really. It's meant to be sung just that way and your bloke was smart enough to see that.'

'Oh, right, thanks, Dad,' I said, mocking him as much as I dared. 'I'll drop Freddy a line, one of the greatest rock singers of all time, and tell him that my father thinks he got something spot-on for once. He'll be chuffed, I'm sure.'

Dad grinned at my sarcasm and to be honest I was feeling a bit lighter than when he came in. But he was wasn't finished yet.

'One of the saddest songs I've ever heard, really. Poor bloke must have been pretty low himself at the time, don't you think?'

'Yeah, pretty low,' I agreed, and wondered why my answer had come so quickly.

'Is anything the matter, Josh? You've been very quiet since you came back from the coast. Anything you want to talk about?'

I shook my head in a textbook imitation of sincerity. 'No, it's like I told Mum. Just tired. We didn't sleep much while we were away.'

'What about your girlfriend? All that seems to have fallen apart.'

'It was time we broke up, you know what I mean.' He was offering me a reason for my moody withdrawal so I added a pathetic little touch. 'I'll get over it, don't worry.'

Dad fell for it and left me alone, but the talk about Alicia set my mind going again and of course thinking about Alicia only made me think about Gemma. The CD was still in the stereo. Dad was right, it was a desperately sad song, sung with bitter understatement. Which was better, Riebolt or Jennings? The comparison appealed to me. Then, with Jennings' spinning under the glass, the words of the chorus finally hit me.

How do the love-broke carry on?
Why does love hurt most when it's gone?

The lines seemed written especially for me, locked in my room as I was, alone and unashamedly self-absorbed. As soon as it was finished I played it through again, listening for the bitter lines each time they came around. I imagined I could feel a physical pain in them and for reasons that didn't come to me until later, I welcomed it. Perhaps some pains are there to remind you what it feels like to be human.

I took my acoustic guitar from the cupboard and experimented with the chords as the tune played over and over. By the time Dad complained about the noise, I'd worked it out, G, D and F mostly with some minor chords at the end of the chorus. I didn't sing the words, but they'd poured into the room so many times by then, I could see them tattooed on the inside of my eyelids.

In those listless days after my return from Mackay, I pictured Clive among the rows of the compactus, and that hidden suitcase. Had he returned any of the items inside it to an ecstatic owner? I thought about visiting him, but I stayed away. Perhaps because of my lethargic spirit, or did his suitcase no longer mean as much to me as it once did?

Dave Zilly rang the morning after Australia Day. 'I'm going to see that doco about Metallica in at the Dendy.'

'Yeah, I'll come.' It was time to get out of the house.

On the way home I stood on the concourse at Central Station with the Lost Property Office sign easy to see at the far end. There were so many people hurrying by, all so ordinary, as I'd once imagined Clive Staples to be, a thousand men and women without much of a life to speak of. What lay inside these people? How did their humanity find a way out into the world?

'You going to see that old guy you worked with?' Dave asked when he came out of the kiosk with a Coke for each of us.

'No, think I'll pass.'

School started again the following week.

'Had any love letters lately, Tambling?' Everyone knew; Alicia's friends had made sure of that.

I couldn't avoid seeing her around the school and tried to be cool about it.

'Hi, how's things?' I asked the first time we were thrown together in a home-room group.

'Much better since I saw through your crap.'

This was going to take time.

Neven was a hassle of a different kind. 'What's happening with the band? Are we getting those speakers?'

I explained about the money, that once I'd paid for my ticket to Mackay and refunded Mike and Kelly for the return, there wasn't enough. He took it well, though he wasn't so pleased when I kept dodging dates for another jam.

'Are you a part of this band or not?' he growled at me one lunch time.

My answer surprised him. 'I don't know!' It surprised me, too.

Then there was Fidelis Day, a Monday this year. Traditionally, the music department takes charge of the concert and since the music teachers were all passengers on Noah's Ark this led to a lot of hands being pressed to delicate brows when the rappers auditioned for a spot on the program or some Year Nine girl sang about wanting a man who was good in bed.

The mummified musos were too busy to bother about stage management and it was just as much a Fidelis tradition that this job fell to Mr Habden.

'I need a team of sound engineers,' he told Neven, Dave and me. 'You, you and you. Be here Sunday, an hour before the rehearsal so we can get the microphones set up and balanced in the assembly hall.' The gruff commands were all part of the Habden charm and we were going to volunteer anyway.

On Sunday Neven settled himself in front of the dials and diodes up in the control room like some high-powered record producer, leaving the grunt work to Dave and me. We were still at it on the stage when the performers started to arrive, cat-nervous and poking their heads in from the foyer.

'Better test those mikes we've set up for the instruments,' Mr Habden announced from floor level in front of us.

A boy had bravely come as far as the centre aisle where he stared at the stage like a condemned prisoner inspecting the scaffold. He hadn't even put down his guitar case when Mr Habden spotted him.

'How 'bout you get up there and play something so we can get the levels right.'

The poor kid looked like he'd been told he was next for the noose. 'No, er, no, I couldn't.'

Mr Habden rolled his eyes and shared a contemptuous smirk with Dave and me. Then, without even drawing breath, he turned the tables on us. 'What about you two? You're both in a band, aren't you?'

We'd been snookered, not that Dave cared whether he looked just as wussy as the boy with the guitar. 'Not me,' he said bluntly.

Oh, what the hell. This was only to get the levels right, anyway.

'Can I use your guitar?' I asked the reluctant performer.

Anything to get himself off the hook. He brought the case to the edge of the stage, opened it quickly and handed the instrument up to me.

'Strum through a song or something, Josh. Hum a bit into the mike, too, if you can. Give us a chance to get the balances right.'

Mr Habden spoke into a mike attached to the headset that kept him in touch with Neven. Looking up, I couldn't see Neven in the control room above the basketball hoop, but I was vaguely aware of more than one figure moving ghost-like behind the darkened glass.

Strum through a song, he'd said. Which song? My fingers explored the neck of the guitar and almost immediately, I hit the strings, all six, in a rich G chord. Why had I picked G? So deep and, to my mind, so melancholy. A tune was taking shape, one I was already humming loud enough to hear.

G, C, Dsus4, D, Dsus2 and D again. I was playing the chords from that Jennings' song. In my room I hadn't been able to let them reverberate with their full range, but there was no reason to hold back here. Mr Habden had retreated to the back of the hall where he signalled for me to keep going. I was coming to the end of the verse: time to switch to the chorus. But I didn't. I was already in position at the microphone and when the moment came, the humming stopped and I began to sing just as my fingers found the first chord of the song.

Close my eyes and try to sleep,
Her face won't let me be.

For those first two lines, I was hearing the two versions inside my head, but the words were so moving and personal that by the time I reached the third I wasn't mimicking the song any more, it had become mine, and right now *I* was singing it, not Don Jennings or Freddy Riebolt, this was Josh Tambling, singing about himself.

Each night I see her in my dreams,
Each night she cuts me free.

I had closed my eyes to concentrate on the right chords because I didn't want to muck them up and have to stop half-way through. The words just flowed out of me in a mournful cascade and if I did stop, they would never come back in quite the same way.

Go on living every day,
Could be for a thousand years.
All the voices asking me,
Questions in my ears.

The chord changes here were quick and I was guessing about the B, but it sounded right. Straight away, I was into the chorus and because my focus was so strongly on the guitar, my voice had to take care of itself.

As I sang, the words cut through me like shattered glass, describing the weeks since my return with a simplicity that made the pain seem white and perfect behind my eyes, a phys-ical pain, like my ribs. '*Why!*' I shouted, as though I wanted everyone in that hall, everyone outside it, too, in fact the whole universe to hear the bitter recrimination that followed, its deepest meaning reserved for me alone.

Does love hurt most when it's gone?

The song kept coming, so intimate now I might have written the words myself. If I could sing them this way then they *were* my words as much as the man who had written them and then died before I was even born. Had he been bound up in his own heartsick misery as I was? Had there been more to Jenning's woes than a lost love, or had he lost faith in so much that he'd been brought up to believe as well? He didn't sound like a particularly happy guy, the little I knew of him. Maybe he thought too much about things, like I did. Maybe he cared.

All the songs I've ever sung,
Can't ease this aching pain.
Form your circles, laughs at me,
Call those lines again.

I was more certain about the chord progression this time and hit the strings hard, working my way through a gradual step down before launching into the chorus again. This wasn't a song now, it was a lament, a confession, another way of crying, a way that didn't have to embarrass me with tears or make those around me cringe as they struggled awkwardly with my private emotion. It didn't matter whether anyone was listening, it was just me. I was singing for myself and I didn't care who heard it as it poured out of me, letting the world know how I felt. It wasn't put on, it wasn't an act. This was my soul reverberating around inside that empty hall and if I opened my eyes, I was sure to see it filling the space like a cloud.

I was almost finished, having sung the saddest song I knew out of the greatest sadness I had ever experienced and yet for a brief instant I was touched by the indescribable ecstasy that had come to me at the end of my dream – not happiness, but a purity of emotion that was no more under my control than my heartbeat.

I opened my eyes and immediately the ecstasy was gone. I didn't regret it, oddly, because the intensity was too much to bear for longer and anyway, it was coming to an end. With my eyes open now, I watched my fingers on the strings and at the final chord, I raised my hand and let the sound die slowly, in its own time.

What a strange moment. I could have wept, but I could just as easily have laughed out loud at the release the song had triggered in me. No song had ever stirred me up like that, not in the singing of it anyway. It had pierced the bitter self-reproach I'd allowed to eat away at me for weeks. There was a kind of triumph in being able to do it like that.

It was done now. I'd sung a song like Mr Habden wanted, to let the rest of his crew play with the controls. He stared silently at me from twenty rows back, his face too far away to read. In fact, the entire hall was strangely quiet in those first few seconds after the final chord fell away, then – applause. There were twenty people at least on either side of Mr Hadben now. Where had they come from? They were all clapping.

I didn't want this. The applause cheapened what had just

happened because I hadn't sung for them, for anyone else at all. I had sung for me.

The clapping continued, much longer than it should have, much longer than polite appreciation of a performance. By the time the applause finally died, like the song, Mr Hadben had come to the front of the stage.

'That was amazing, Josh. Fabulous. An old Don Jennings' song, isn't it?'

I nodded, to the question about Jennings, anyway.

'I had no idea that my star history pupil was such a talent. Are you going to sing that tomorrow?'

Sing it tomorrow! What was he talking about? I was part of the sound crew. 'I'm not on the program,' I pointed out, sheepishly.

'That can be fixed,' he replied with a wink.

Some of the impromptu audience had drifted towards the stage, too, listening to Mr Habden as they came. 'Yeah, that was great. You should do that in the concert,' said a girl I vaguely recognised from the year below me. 'Wish I could sing like that,' she added to a friend beside her.

Had I sung that well! I was beginning to feel uncomfortable. I jumped down from the stage and handed the guitar back to its owner who looked even more distraught about his own performance now.

Dave was there as well, though, and being Dave he had just the remark to make my heart cringe. 'Oh, mate, sing that song tomorrow and Alicia will beg you to take her back.'

Alicia! What the hell was he talking about? But as I stood

appalled by his gawky, suggestive grin, the meaning hit me harder than those two thieves in Brisbane. He thought I had been singing about Alicia and if I got up on that stage tomorrow and performed in front of the whole school, they would all think the same, even Alicia herself.

'No,' I said. 'No way. It's personal.'

Dave wasn't giving up just yet and found an ally when Neven arrived, saying, 'Josh, that was unbelievable. Mate, the way you sang just then . . . I take it all back, what I said about not connecting with the audience. Gemma said the same thing.'

'Gemma!'

'Yeah, she came by to see how it was going. She was up in the control box with me just now. She was watching you like a hawk and even before you'd finished she was saying, 'See what Josh can do when he wants to? He's much better when he's not screaming his lungs out.'

'Gemma was there, in the control box, listening!' I repeated.

'Yeah, and I swear you put a tear in her eye, mate.'

'Where is she now?

'As soon you finished she had to go.'

'There was a call for you, Josh,' Mum announced when I arrived home from the rehearsal. 'A girl. Said she would call back later.'

News can make lightning look slow when girls are armed with mobile phones and my first thought was that Alicia had heard I was singing love songs to win her back. One part of me already wished I hadn't got up there on that stage and done what I did, yet another part of me wouldn't take those moments back for a stack of platinum records. There was a moment towards the end when I sensed an exquisite melancholy arching across me, with all my emotions separated out like the colours of a rainbow. It left a residue that hummed through me still. No, I didn't regret singing that song, whatever happened as a result.

I had been home for half an hour when the phone rang again.

'Josh, it's the same girl,' Mum called from the kitchen. 'Says her name is Gemma.'

She met me in the hallway with the phone, which I took back to my room. Damn this body of mine; my heart was going like an Olympic sprinter's, making me so light-headed I had to sit on the edge of my bed and take a couple of deep breaths before I put the phone to my ear.

'Hello?'

'Josh, it's me,' she began, assuming with total confidence that I would recognise her voice. 'I had to call after the way you sang that song this afternoon.'

'I didn't know you were there, Gemma. That's the truth. If I'd known, I wouldn't have sung like that.'

'Why not, Josh? It was the most fantastic thing I've ever heard. No one ever sings like that at a concert. They might pretend that everything they're singing about is going on inside them, but it's just an act. You can tell when they smile and take a bow at the end. That wasn't what you did today. It was a one off, wasn't it, Josh. I was glad I was there to see it, so glad.'

'Look, Gemma, I know you're with Neven. I wasn't trying to change your mind or anything, believe me.'

'I know that, Josh. You didn't even know I was there. This call hasn't got anything to do with Neven and me. This is about you, Josh. I'm ringing because I saw what was happening to you down there on the stage. Singing that way . . . you were singing from inside yourself, Josh, for the first time that I've ever seen, and I'll bet it was the first time anyone else has seen it, too. In our garage, you only ever sang what the guys wanted you to sing and always the way they wanted you to sing it. Oh, Josh, what came out of you today was so honest and so real I could almost see it.'

I didn't know what to make of this and like an idiot, I let an awkward silence echo down the line.

'I've got to go, Josh, okay? I just wanted to tell you . . . what I just said, okay?'

'I've got to go, too,' I said. 'Thanks for calling me like this . . . and for saying those things. Bye.'

I lay down on my good side, staring at the silent phone in my hand. What had all that been about? Gemma was certainly adamant: it wasn't about her and Neven or the way I had mucked up my chance to be with her. All that was long passed. She had seen something in me this afternoon, even used much the same words to describe it. 'You were singing from inside yourself, Josh. The first time anyone has ever seen it.' Had Gemma glimpsed the precious item I went looking for on those trains? Hours and hours of searching, when all the time it was coursing through every inch of me, like blood.

I had only felt an emotion like that once before, on the bus at the end of my dream. It wasn't happiness, it wasn't sadness either, it was a moment when I felt a goodness in me, present and undeniable. Even as I worked it out, that presence came to me again, a warmth, an afterglow. Such a fleeting thing, it was already gone, but it was enough to know what it was now and that it was a part of me.

There was a lightness, too. I was a ten-year-old, walking on the beach with my family and happy in a way that doesn't translate into words. I was younger still, a kid playing in his

253

Roman soldier's outfit, lost in imagination and without the self-consciousness that crowds out the joy of living. For weeks, maybe months, I had been deeply inside my own thoughts and I was tired of it, so tired. There was a way out now and this was where that lightness was drawing me.

I wanted to tell someone. Gemma? Even as the thought took shape in my mind, I dismissed it. She had done as much as I could ask already and the awkward way we had ended our conversation was warning enough. My restlessness grew steadily, too much to let me play my guitar. Even my stack of CDs wouldn't do it for me this time. I was sitting up, eager to get out of my claustrophobic bedroom when there was a knock on my door.

'Josh?'

'I'm here,' I called.

The door opened and moments later Dad's head appeared round the edge. 'We're going to mass at five, all right?'

This was a reminder he had given me a hundred times before, to which I invariably replied, 'Yeah', or 'Okay'. This time I said nothing, but simply stared at his disembodied head.

He must have noticed something was wrong because he straightened up and let the door swing open further until his entire body was revealed in the doorway. He didn't come in. During the last year or so, without ever discussing the matter, he'd started to ask permission before he entered my territory.

'Dad, can I speak to you for a minute?'

'Sure,' he said, but he still didn't move.

I shoved myself back further onto the bed until I felt the

solid wall behind me, at the same time glancing towards the swivel chair at my desk. He took the hint and finally entered the room and lowered himself into the chair. 'What's up?'

'I sang that song at the rehearsal today, to help Mr Habden get the sound levels right.'

He didn't have a clue what I was talking about.

'The one Don Jennings sings with just a guitar.'

His face loosened its creases. '*Love-broke.*'

'Yeah, that one. It went over really well. There's something about that song that gets to me. They were all saying I should do it again in the concert tomorrow.'

Poor Dad. Here was his son, already the same height as him, and sounding like an eight-year-old telling his father about the hat trick of tries he'd scored in a footy game.

'What I'm saying is, thanks for that song. It meant something special to me, the lyrics were just right but Gemma was there and she rang here just now to say that it wasn't an act . . .'

Shut up, Josh! None of this was making any sense to Dad because he didn't have the faintest idea of the decisions I'd made over the last few months. So I stopped trying to tell him about the rehearsal this afternoon and I told him something else instead. 'Dad, I'm not going to church tonight.'

His eyes locked onto mine. Despite all my rambling, he knew exactly what I was telling him, that I was announcing a lot more than those simple words implied.

'What's the matter, Josh?'

I'd stopped thinking about consequences, about who was

going to be hurt, upset, angry. 'Dad, I can't pretend any more. I just don't believe there's a God watching over us, listening to our prayers, expecting us to live up to his rules.'

He raised his eyebrows, leaving his face pensive and solemn, but apart from that he didn't seem to make any response at all. I couldn't leave it at that, not after all the hours I had sat and stood and knelt beside him in our parish church, working out what made sense to me and what didn't. I started to tell him, expecting him to go off the handle, watching his eyes carefully to judge when the moment would come. But when he finally broke into my avalanche of words it was with the simplest of statements.

'It's a matter of faith, Josh.'

This was probably the only thing we agreed about any more. Those few words meant we had reached the crossroads in all of this, where he stood facing in one direction and I'd taken the first step in another. An uncomfortable silence fell between us, broken only when he shifted in the seat, making it complain under his weight. His eyes left mine to focus indeterminately somewhere between his knee and the floor. 'You've obviously thought about this for quite a long time.' After another lengthy pause he leaned forward with his elbows on his knees and raised his face to look straight into mine. 'You haven't just drifted away out of indifference, like Michael did. It must have been hard, keeping it to yourself until now.'

Yes, so hard. The way he'd said that, holding me with his eyes more powerfully than his hands could have gripped my shoulders, set me free all over again. I started talking, more easily this time.

'That job you got me at the Lost Property Office, Dad. That's where I found the photo and if I hadn't . . .' The words died in my throat just in time. 'Clive has this suitcase where he saves things the rest of us would throw away,' I said instead and before I knew it I was telling Dad about the little scheme Clive had going to help out people that no one else would ever think of helping – and of the joy it brought them. I told him how I'd tried to hitch a ride on Clive's quiet caring and what it had done to me, even the truth about that Friday when I ended up on Cronulla Station, staring at the stars and more lost myself than anything I would ever find abandoned on a train.

'All that thinking I did in church left me empty. I was worried that there wasn't anything of me left, that if I didn't believe in God then I mustn't have a soul either. But that's wrong, Dad, so wrong.' How did I tell him about the moment in Mackay when Mike spoke to Mum? How did I tell him about my dream? He was already staring at me, stunned by the passionate way I was explaining all this. If I started quoting my dreams, he'd think I was crazy.

'I've worked out what the soul is, you see. It's the good inside us. God or no God, the soul's a human thing.'

'Hey, you two. Time to get ready.'

Mum's interruption was like an axe slicing the rope that tied us together. Dad reeled back in the chair and stared at her for a moment as though he didn't recognise her.

'Mass,' she reminded him. 'It's twenty to five.'

He came to himself quickly, stood up and shuffled towards her before hesitating in the doorway where Mum blocked his exit.

'You too, Josh,' she insisted when I didn't move.

'No,' said Dad firmly. 'Josh isn't coming with us.'

'What do you mean?' Mum demanded, looking with narrowed eyes towards me.

'It's all right, Carol,' he said, ushering her into the hall. 'It's Josh's choice. He's decided to go his own way.'

That wasn't the end of it. Dad and I were talking in the car again, even during my driving lessons when I should have been concentrating on the road. (Nearly put us under a truck on the Harbour Bridge.) God copped a mention occasionally but mostly it was other stuff, even football when St George started trial games for the new season, and if one of us really wanted to stir up the other, we'd go on about music.

I'd more or less left the band after Mackay. Musical differences. The guys did Dave's cousin's eighteenth birthday without me and I heard it didn't go so well. Of course, there was another reason why I'd gone cold on the band: the Kominsky garage was still jam-central.

The best thing, though, was the noise in our house again, not necessarily the kind of noise you could hear, though with a sister like Hayley there were always plenty of squeals and complaints and banging doors. You might call it background noise, a kind of hum, like insects, like the life of a city creating its own static, yes, that's it, like a dormant city come back to life.

Hayley heard that static too. 'The radio was on in the kitchen when I came home this afternoon,' she told me while gorging carbos before squad training.

Mike phoned about once a fortnight, and if he still rang at dinner time, it wasn't so he'd catch me at home, it was because Mum was sure to be there. 'It's Michael,' she called the first time that I was there to see it. She didn't push her luck, not that time or during any of the calls afterwards, she never said, 'Michael, your father's here.' I guess she didn't want to jeopardise what she had and who could blame her? The odd thing was that I began to feel left out. Talk about ironic! After all that time I'd spent dreading the sound of Mike's voice on the line and hating my role as the go-between, now I didn't get a chance to speak to him at all.

Then, during the second or third call – I know it was the eighteenth of February – Mum suddenly handed me the phone. 'He wants to speak to you.'

'Hi, Josh, how you doin'?' said the voice I hadn't heard since leaving Mackay. 'I suppose Mum's still there listening, is she?'

'Yep.'

'Well, go out onto the deck for a second. Somewhere private.'

'Okay, I'll go check,' I said, as though he'd asked me to report some vague detail he needed. Down the hall, into my room. 'I'm alone. What's up?'

'Can't you guess? Kelly's had the baby!'

'You're joking!' I let out a mighty whoop. 'Boy or girl?'

'Keep your voice down, you dimwit. They didn't hear you, did they?' he hissed.

My voice became a contrite whisper. 'Don't think so.'

'Just as well. Anyway, it's a boy,' and after this blunt announcement, my brother's excitement grew with every word. 'You're an uncle. Can you believe it, Josh, I've got a son!'

Mum greeted me with a suspicious eye when I put the phone back in its cradle. 'What was all the yelling about?'

'Secret brothers' business.'

A sceptical snort challenged this evasion but after Mike's call, her mood was too light-hearted to care. My brother was still two thousand kilometres from home and officially Mum and Dad didn't know where he was, but really we were now just another family with one of its members living and working a long way from home.

Two days after that call Dad and I slipped down to Kogarah to watch St George get creamed by Canterbury in the pre-season comp. Dates were on my mind. My new nephew would have the eighteenth as his birthday but today was the day Mike had met Kelly in that pub, exactly a year ago.

'Dad, when did you get the report about Mike from the private detective?'

'February last year.'

'Yeah, but when in February.'

'Why's it so important, Josh?' He winced as the Bulldogs went in for another try, but when I kept at him he came up with the goods. 'It was the week Hayley started at Fidelis.'

'First week then.'

He nodded, still perplexed. He had no idea what that answer meant but I did and already my stomach was churning. If Dad had flown to Mackay as soon as he'd found out where Michael was, if he'd convinced him to come home, willingly or not, Michael and Kelly would never have met.

I nearly threw up. To think that I'd been so angry with him when he hadn't gone up there to bring Michael home. The urge to tell him became an ache in my chest far worse than broken ribs.

Without the band, I was restless. Old habits die hard and though there was no one to play them with, I taught myself a few songs off the radio, songs I liked, picking out the music with my acoustic guitar the way I used to with Neven. Then, early in March, Dave came round to see me.

'None of us can sing, you dopey bastard. We need you.'

'I don't know, Dave, the kind of material Neven's into, it doesn't suit me.'

'Stuff Neven! He's had it all his own way for too long. He's nothing but a bloody show-pony, anyway. You're the one, Josh, you've always been the guts of this band.'

Where was this coming from? 'Are you serious?'

'Of course I am, and Gemma says the same. She's been on at Neven about it, herself. After the way you sang at the rehearsal, even he's had a rethink. Not that he'll say so. Come on, Josh, with you back at the microphone, we'll go places, I can feel it.'

So Dave Zilly stitched the band back together. Who would have believed it? We're still developing our new material and don't get the wrong idea – as a band we're still a lot closer to Pearl Jam than Barry Manilow – but the restlessness has mostly gone. I've even written a few songs myself.

I see Gemma at rehearsals and we talk more easily every time. Things are still going well between her and Neven. I've got my eye on a girl at Fidelis, too, her name's Isobelle and gradually, through those first months of the year, my life seemed to be mending along with my broken ribs.

Then Mike came home.

It was Good Friday, the first day of the Easter long week-end. Hayley was onto the phone like a hawk in case it was one of her girlfriends. She stood there with the cordless in her hand saying, 'It's Michael, he wants to speak to Dad.'

You should have seen the look on Mum's face. She took the phone from Hayley. 'Michael? Look, Dad's gone down to Kogarah Oval, something to do with the game tomorrow.'

The phone squawked as Mike told her something and then Mum yelled out, 'The airport! What, here in Sydney?'

There was more talking, but all Hayley and I could hear was Mum's end of the conversation. 'Yes, of course you can come and stay. Stay as long as you like. Oh, just for Easter, yes, that's fine. We'll come and get you. No? Oh, okay then, we'll be here. How long will it take? Dad? I'll call him. He'll be here when you arrive, don't worry about that. Oh, Michael . . .'

The call was over. Mum just stood there staring at Hayley

and me. 'He's at the airport. He's getting a taxi. Be here in half an hour. He says he's bringing a surprise to show us.'

That was just how my brother would do it. He decides to come home after two-and-a-half years and he gives them thirty minutes notice. I don't think Mum was thinking that way. The zombie stare was leaving her face and Mum, the organiser, was kicking her way back into the cockpit.

'Your father!' The cordless still in her hand, she stabbed the numbers that would have Dad's mobile trilling away with that tinny bit of the William Tell Overture. 'Phil, Phil, Michael just called. He's in Sydney. He's on his way here now. Yes, yes, I'm serious. He was on the phone just a minute ago. He asked for you, Phil. He wanted to speak to you.'

She didn't need to order him home. Ten minutes later the Statesman was in the driveway. Mum had sent Hayley and me to clear our junk out of the room downstairs while she did a quick tidy-up of the lounge room. Then she and Dad attacked Michael's old room like twin tornadoes before joining Hayley and me on the verandah where we could see any car that turned into our street.

'No sign of a taxi yet,' said Hayley.

We waited, not saying much. Hayley picked up the nervous vibes Mum and Dad gave off like an electrical charge and began to dance from one foot to the other until Mum snapped at her to stop.

'Thirty minutes,' said Dad. 'Add another fifteen if he had to stand in line for a cab.'

With forty minutes gone since the call, I couldn't stand the waiting and went downstairs into the front yard. The others followed me until we ended up standing in a line across the grass, like the reception line at a wedding. Or a firing squad.

'There it is. He's coming!' Hayley cried when the taxi turned the corner. As it pulled into the kerb, my sister rushed forward and I went after her. Mum and Dad didn't move.

If I'd stopped for two seconds I might have guessed Michael wouldn't come alone, and of course Kelly didn't have that big round bump under her dress any more. As Mike helped her out of the car, she was holding a tiny baby in her arms.

'Hi ya, Hayley,' my brother was saying. 'Hey, look at the size of you. You're so tall.'

He had to pay the driver and there were the bags to get out of the boot. That left Kelly alone on the footpath, in an awkward moment as Hayley stared at Kelly and the little thing in her arms. Hayley's eyes were out on stalks.

Then Kelly saw me, a few metres back on the grass. Oh, here we go! If she called out to me, making it obvious that we'd already met, Mum and Dad would want to know how. But she didn't call my name, in fact, she didn't keep her eyes on me for long at all. She was staring up at Mum and Dad as they came across the grass towards her.

The taxi pulled away, leaving Mike with the bags on the curb. 'Josh, can you help with these?' When I hurried round behind Kelly to join him, he whispered, 'Don't worry, mate. We're not going to say how you came for a visit.' He stopped and looked me in the eye. 'We'll tell them one day, though, when they're grown-up enough to handle it.'

A nice way to put it, but before I could tell him so, he had left me to go and stand beside his little family.

'Mum and Dad, this is Kelly,' he said proudly, 'and this one here,' he added, tugging gently at the baby's rucked-up jacket so we could all see the little face, 'this is your grandson, Stuart.'

Mum burst like fireworks over the Harbour Bridge. 'A grandson! Oh, Michael, why didn't you say? Not a word of warning and suddenly I'm a grandmother.'

'You'll have to start dyeing your hair grey,' he teased, but Mum wasn't biting, not today. She held out her arms towards Kelly, demanding her due as a grandma. The little bundle passed from mother to mother. 'It's such a shock, the best shock I've had in my entire life!'

The word 'beautiful' got a thorough working-over in the babble that followed. Once Mum had run through the quiz about birthweight and how many weeks old Stuart was, she wedged him expertly in one arm and reached out with the other to embrace Kelly. 'It's so wonderful to have you here. We were expecting one person in the taxi. Three is . . . well, it's three times as good.'

So what if Mum was getting soppy. Dad was standing on the edge of the family huddle, excluded for the moment by the greater excitement of Mum and Hayley and Mike who was so proud and hey, I was in the middle of that scrum, too, getting my share.

Slowly, the first flush of exhilaration died down and that was when Mike stepped away and stood face to face with Dad.

He held out his hand and said, 'I'm sorry I didn't let you know where I was. It was a mongrel thing to do.'

Dad glanced at me for the briefest second then back at my brother. Maybe there were some things Mike would find out when he was old enough to handle them, too.

After that momentary hesitation, Dad took Mike's hand and shook it. 'I'm just glad you've come home.'

'It's only for Easter. We've got to fly back on Monday afternoon. I'm working on a trawler out of Mackay. Got to be on board by six. Maybe you and Mum can come up and see us. We're renting at the moment, but the owner wants to sell and I'm talking to the bank. You never know, everything's much cheaper up there.'

Mike had been speaking very quickly, but now he stopped because he knew he had to say something else before any of this could mean much. 'I was always going to come home, Dad. There were just some things I had to do first.'

'So I see,' my father replied with a wry grin. 'Congratulations, Mike, he's a beautiful little boy.'

'There was more to it than Stuart, Dad,' and here my brother's voice faltered. 'Lots more,' he managed, before falling silent altogether.

Come on, Mike, I urged him beneath the same silence. Tell him what you told me up there in Mackay. No, nothing. But Dad simply nodded and in that instant it didn't seem to matter: all the pain each time Michael had called and spoken to me alone and then later, just to Mum. It was all gone in a handshake.

What Mike had said was true, he was always going to come back. It didn't matter whether I had gone to Mackay or not. He came back to show us the baby, and Kelly of course. He brought back a lot more than he took away with him and none of that was because of me.

While I was thinking this, Mum turned towards us with the baby in her arms and a joy in her face like I'd seen once before, in my first week at the Lost Property Office. 'Here,' she said, lifting the baby towards Dad. 'You take your grandson for a minute while I give Michael a proper hug.'

So Dad took the baby in his arms and stood there watching as Mum threw her arms around Mike. For a few moments, tears welled in Dad's eyes and rolled down his cheeks and with his hands full, he couldn't wipe them away.

'Oh, Phil, look at you,' Mum laughed when she saw them. Dad gave her a strangled, helpless look but he wasn't embarrassed.

Mum moved to Dad's side for another peek at their grandson. Kelly followed and Mike, too, and Hayley was well and truly over her shyness of this brother she had begun to forget.

'Give Hayley a nurse,' said Mum.

'In a minute, Carol, in a minute,' Dad replied and he went on holding little Stuart while Mike wiped away a streak of curdled milk dribbling from the baby's lips.

I was in there with them, carrying in my head the secrets that remained between Mike and my parents and the truths that might have been revealed. Would they make any difference?

Mum had the precious thing she craved and as for Dad, what he needed to know, he already knew. He had taken a father's risk, and it had paid off.

The weight of this felt good in my chest, so good. Nothing stood between me and the joy coming out. I'd wanted to feel this way with Clive in the Lost Property Office, helping other people find what they had lost, but that was never going to work. I had to find what was lost within me before it could happen.

It happened that day, when my brother came home. I was happy that day.